Amber's hiding a desperate secret . . .

Pain shot through my legs, my ankles, my feet. Moaning and crying, I hobbled my way into the shower.

As the hot water cascaded over my painful joints, I could feel the pain easing and some mobility returning. After ten minutes, the hot water ran out, but I was feeling much better. So I really had just overdone my workout my first day up after the flu. That's all it was. That's all I'd let it be.

I moved slowly getting dressed, but at least I could move. I popped three aspirin and soon felt myself sweating out my low-grade fever. I felt tired and weak, but I was ready when Richmond pulled up to drive me to school.

On the outside, I looked completely normal. As the day progressed, no one knew that I felt like falling over with exhaustion, that just holding a pen to write made my fingers scream with pain, that when I walked it felt as if someone were driving burning needles into my heels. No one knew. And I wasn't going to let any

Did You Hear About Amber?

Did You Hear About Amber?

by Cherie Bennett

PUFFIN BOOKS

PUFFIN BOOKS
Published by the Penguin Group
Penguin Books USA Inc., 375 Hudson Street, New York, New York 10014, U.S.A.
Penguin Books Ltd, 27 Wrights Lane, London W8 5TZ, England
Penguin Books Australia Ltd, Ringwood, Victoria, Australia
Penguin Books Canada Ltd, 10 Alcorn Avenue, Toronto, Ontario, Canada M4V 3B2
Penguin Books (N.Z.) Ltd, 182–190 Wairau Road, Auckland 10, New Zealand

Penguin Books Ltd, Registered Offices: Harmondsworth, Middlesex, England

First published in the United States of America by Puffin Books,
a division of Penguin Books USA Inc., 1993

1 3 5 7 9 10 8 6 4 2

LIBRARY OF CONGRESS CATALOGING-IN-PUBLICATION DATA
Bennett, Cherie.
Did you hear about Amber? / Cherie Bennett.
p.   cm.—(Surviving sixteen; #1) (A Puffin high flyer)
Summary: Manipulative sixteen year old Amber, a talented dancer,
sees her future threatened when she feels the crippling effects of
rheumatoid arthritis.
ISBN 0-14-036318-1
[1. Rheumatoid arthritis—Fiction.   2. Physically handicapped—
Fiction.   3. Dancing—Fiction.]   I. Title.   II. Series.
III. Series: Bennett, Cherie. Surviving sixteen: #1.
PZ7.B43912D1 1993   [Fic]—dc20   92-42428   CIP   AC

Printed in the United States of America

This book is for my mom,
Roslyn Ozur Cantor

The author wishes to thank rheumatologist extraordinaire Dr. John Sergent and teen extraordinaire Julia McFerrin, both of Nashville, Tennessee, for their assistance with this book.

Did You Hear About Amber?

CHAPTER ONE

On the first day of my junior year of high school, I made Richmond Remington the Third kiss me right in front of Suzanne Lafayette's locker.

Of course I knew Suzanne would be there, picking up her chemistry book, which is exactly why I did it. All of sophomore year and most of the summer, Richmond—I call him Richie just because I know he hates it—had been *Suzanne's* boyfriend. Everyone said they were perfect together. Richmond's family is old money—they've got more millions than they can count—and Suzanne's family does, too. On top of that, they're both smart, and really good-looking in that nauseating preppie sort of way.

In August, I'd decided to make him mine.

It was almost too easy.

I knew Richmond would be at the Bellevue Mall on Saturday, where his best friend Jackson had a summer job at Sam Goody's. I wore a white lace mini, short enough to make him drool but long enough to make him use his imagination, an oversized white T-shirt, and some French perfume Momma'd received from one of her so-called gentlemen callers. I sprayed that perfume through my long, naturally wavy blonde hair and shook my head 'til my hair was real wild-looking. Then I outlined my eyes with thick black eyeliner, put on false eyelashes, and that was it. No other makeup. I looked kind of like a young Marilyn Monroe. Only better.

"Hey, Richmond," I drawled as I sashayed into the record store and idly perused the latest CDs.

"Hey, Amber," Richmond said easily. "How's your summer been?"

"Hot." I looked him dead in the eye.

"Yeah, well, that's Nashville in the summer for you," he replied good-naturedly. "Good thing the whole world is air-conditioned now, huh?"

"Not the dance studio where we rehearse," I told him. "Air conditioning is bad for dancers."

"That a fact," Richmond said politely.

"Dancers are supposed to stay hot," I told him. "It's good for the muscles."

I flexed my tanned leg and saw his Adam's apple bob as he thought about all those various hot muscles of mine. Then I stretched my arms languidly over my head. "I could really use a massage," I said, arching my back. I looked him over, head to foot and back up again. "Do you give good massages?"

"I've been known to," he grinned. Evidently the image of the pristine Suzanne Lafayette swam into his mind at just that moment, because he added, "At least Suzanne says I do."

"How could she really tell, though," I mused, "through all her clothes?" This was a calculated guess on my part. I figured Suzanne Lafayette probably *bathed* in a color-coordinated ensemble.

"That's true," Richmond agreed thoughtfully.

"Well, I'm rehearsing this afternoon until five," I told him, "and I'll be dying for a massage right about then." I picked up one of his hands and placed it just below my collar bone. "Do you feel a knot there?"

"No," he said huskily.

"I think you could probably feel it if I took off this heavy T-shirt, though," I said seriously.

"Oh, yeah," he breathed, images of me minus my T-shirt undoubtedly dancing through his head.

"Could you be a lifesaver and come by the dance studio at five?" I asked him, still holding his hand in mine.

"I might could do that," he said, his head bobbing up and down on his neck just like those little dogs in the back of tacky people's cars.

"Aren't you sweet," I told him, giving him back his hand. "I know by then I'll just be *panting* for some relief." With that, I waved bye-bye and walked away. I could feel his eyes still on me as I headed around the corner.

It was like taking candy from a baby.

Naturally Richmond showed up at five, and naturally I was wearing my hot pink leotard with the high-cut legs, the tiny little spaghetti straps, and no back. That meant he could massage my naked flesh without my removing a single garment. I didn't even let him kiss me (which made him wild with desire). I told him I couldn't possibly, as long as he belonged to someone else. Within a week he'd broken up with Suzanne, and I'd been riding in the bucket seat of his hot red Miata convertible ever since.

As Richmond finished kissing me, I caught Suzanne's eye and gave her a triumphant little grin. She banged her locker shut and stomped off down the hall.

"I'll meet you in the parking lot at three," Richmond told me before he headed off to class.

"Not today," I said. "I'm holding auditions for Sizzle, remember?"

Richmond knew what Sizzle was. Everyone at school did. It was the dance trio I'd started the year before. We'd already appeared in clubs around Nashville, and had won a regional contest in Atlanta. We danced to rock, rap, and hip-hop music, and we were great. But one of the girls had moved, so I was picking a new girl to replace her.

"I'll come watch, then," Richmond said, nuzzling my neck.

"Whatever." I shrugged, and walked away.

You have to understand, the key with Richmond was never to act like I cared very much. Since every girl in our class was so obviously lusting after him, I had to be different to stand out from the crowd.

But then, I always have stood out from the crowd.

For example: I'm not sure if this is a real

memory or I just think I remember it because Momma's told me the story so much. For my third birthday Momma got me this little pink dress that was all lace and frills. It was someone's throw-away, which Momma got at the Goodwill. But she fixed it up really nice, and I didn't know the difference. I remember dancing around in that beautiful dress—I wouldn't even take it off to sleep—and Momma exclaiming, "You are the prettiest, smartest, most talented girl in the world!"

I believed her.

By the time I was five, I was making up dances to the music on TV, radio, whatever, which I would teach to Momma. By the time I was seven, I was organizing beauty pageants in our neighborhood, just because I knew I'd always win. By the time I was ten, without ever taking a dance lesson in my life, *I* was charging girls fifty cents to take dance lessons from *me*.

But the ultimate achievement, as far as Momma was concerned, was getting a full scholarship to the Covington School when I was fourteen-going-on-fifteen. You would have thought she'd died and gone to heaven, she was so happy.

Covington is this very ritzy private school for kids who are artistic, smart, and rich.

Covington also prides itself on being egalitarian, so they give scholarships to a few select kids who are artistic, smart, and poor. That's me. There are three scholarship students in each grade. But if a kid gets in when he was, say, ten years old, he keeps his spot unless his grade point average falls below 3.0.

When I applied at the end of ninth grade, there was only one full scholarship spot open for the tenth grade class. Now, I had a 3.8 average at my public school, which believe me, wasn't so difficult to do. But I figured they had lots of kids applying who had grades that high, or even higher, so I knew I had to do something to stand out in their minds. So I showed up for the interview and danced an original dance I had choreographed to Anton Dvořák's "New World" Symphony. I told them that the dance represented *my* new world, where there were no poor girls like me. I wore strategically torn rags for a costume and tried to look pathetic. They ate it up with a spoon.

From my very first day at Covington, I had a

plan. I was going to become the coolest, most popular girl in the school. It was bad enough I was poor, which nobody but nobody was going to find out if I could help it. I couldn't settle for even second best. I had to be number one.

It helped that I got picked head cheerleader, even though I was new. Some girls whispered that it wasn't fair, but I was clearly the best, so there wasn't really anything to complain about. Then when I started Sizzle and we started to get actual paying gigs around town, my popularity was assured. Now I had Richmond, too.

"Amber, what should I wear to the Sizzle audition?" Bitsy Renfrey asked me as I slipped into my seat in the bio lab.

"Doesn't matter to me," I said coolly, tossing the hair off my face.

"But I mean, what would be right?" she asked anxiously, chewing on her lower lip.

I sighed. Bitsy Renfrey had frizzy hair and was shaped like a pear. She clearly was not Sizzle material. "A leotard or something," I finally said, opening my biology book to shut her up. Somewhat forlornly, Bitsy trudged off to her seat.

"*She's* auditioning?" Lindsey Van Owen whispered from behind me. Lindsey is a cheerleader, very cute, very cool.

"On Broadway they weed people out so you don't even have to audition the ones who are hopeless," I whispered back. "It's called a cattle call."

"*Cattle* is right," Lindsey said, raising her eyebrows at Bitsy's thunder thighs. "Moo-oo-oo!"

"Hey, Amber, your skirt looks great," Donna Martin said, sliding into the seat next to me. Donna was in Sizzle with me, and was my best friend. She'd gone shopping with me for the skirt the week before school started.

"Thanks," I said. The skirt was short, straight denim with black leather pockets, and with it I wore a sleeveless ribbed black T-shirt with a mock turtleneck. I'd saved every penny I made teaching aerobics over the summer at The Gym, the hippest workout place in town, so that I could buy some new clothes for school. Donna spent ten times as much as I did on that little shopping spree, but then all Donna had to do was to hand over her daddy's credit card.

"Everyone in school is talking about the Sizzle auditions," Donna said, pushing her straight black hair behind one diamond-studded ear. "I saw girls actually practicing dance routines in the john just now!"

"Welcome to Advanced Biology," Mr. St. John said from the front of the room. "Let's start with the diagram on page one, shall we?"

I got through Advanced Biology and American Literature, and then I dashed across the street to The Gym, where the Sizzle auditions were being held. Crater Owens (his real name is Creeter, but he earned the nickname Crater as a teenager because of his terrible skin) waved to me from the StairMaster, where he was supervising the workout of a nervous-looking fat woman. Crater owns the gym, and he had a huge crush on me. That's why he let me use the back dance studio for free whenever there wasn't a class.

"Hey, Amber-Lynn," Crater called, walking into the dance studio a few minutes later. "You need any help?"

"No thanks," I said, going through my tapes to find the cassettes I wanted for the audition.

"Well, if'n you do, you just give a holler, you hear?" he said.

I winced at his voice. He has one of those real hick-sounding southern accents that I cannot stand. My mother sounds the same way. Although Crater has made himself over into a muscle-bound fool and his skin has pretty much cleared up so you can see how good-looking he really is, that white-trash accent of his ruined the whole package.

"I'll just leave this for you, then," Crater said, setting a frosty bottle of Perrier by my feet like a love offering. He knew it was my favorite.

Soon the studio filled up with girls tittering nervously about the audition, and with guys who wanted to gawk at the girls.

"More girls are trying out for this than tried out for cheerleader," Donna said, as she tied her hair back with a bandana. She pulled off her denim skirt. Underneath she was wearing the same outfit I was wearing, which was one of our three stage outfits: black leotard with Day-Glo lightning bolts across the front, and black Lycra biker shorts. Underneath the biker shorts we wore black fishnets, with black, hightop sneakers completing the look.

"Let's audition them to 'Buff Enough,' " I decided, pulling my favorite cassette from the pile.

"It took me and Missy forever to learn that one," Donna exclaimed.

"Exactly," I replied. "I don't want to waste my time."

"Hey, baby," Richmond said, coming up behind me and planting a kiss on my shoulder.

"I'm working, Richie," I said coolly.

"Too busy for me, huh?" he said in a mocking voice.

"That's right," I answered.

"Oh, you are *so* tough," he teased, his hand running down my back. I gave him a sexy grin and then slapped his hand away. He walked across the room and sat down with three of his friends.

"Okay, listen up!" I told the forty or so girls who sat waiting to audition. "Donna and I are going to show ya'll a dance combination, and then you'll do it in groups of four. We're looking for one great dancer with great style who learns real fast."

I flipped the switch on the cassette player, and the sounds of "Buff Enough" filled the room. Donna and I danced the first sixteen bars full out, after which the girls applauded and the guys whistled and hooted.

After that we broke the dance down into beats and taught it to the girls. Some of them picked it up quickly, most of them didn't. Donna counted them off into groups of four while I rewound the tape.

After everyone danced, Donna and I huddled for a moment, picking out the few girls who might have any hope. We narrowed it down to eight.

"These eight girls please stay," I called out. "The rest of you can leave or stay and watch." When I finished reading the list, I looked up and saw the disappointment etched on the faces of some of the girls whose names hadn't been on the list. Bitsy Renfrey looked crushed.

"I can't believe Bitsy expected to get this," Donna said, looking across the room at Bitsy's crestfallen face.

"Actually, she's a really good dancer," I said, looking over the finalists list.

"Well, yeah," Donna agreed, "but we couldn't have a girl with that big ole bod in Sizzle!"

"Yeah," Lindsey agreed, overhearing Donna. "You'd have to change the name to Fizzle!"

That cracked Donna and Lindsey up. Lindsey was Donna's other best friend. I thought she was kind of obnoxious, myself.

Donna and I watched carefully as the eight

finalists danced their hearts out, then we huddled to discuss what we thought.

"Lindsey's the best, I think," Donna said.

"She's good," I agreed, "but Cassie has more style and a better body."

"Cassie Stewart?" Donna moaned. "She didn't even make cheerleader!"

"She didn't try out for cheerleader, and you know it," I said. I looked over at Cassie, who was leaning against the window ledge, looking totally self-confident. She had red hair that waved over one eye like a movie star from the forties. As far as I was concerned, she was the second coolest girl at Covington School, and now I knew she was also a really great dancer.

"Cassie Stewart is too much of a snot to take direction from you," Donna warned.

"Hey, she just did," I pointed out. I looked at Lindsey and then at Cassie. No contest.

I turned to face the group. "Thanks for auditioning," I told them. "We'll call the girl we picked tonight."

Lindsey shot Donna a look, and Donna looked away. Cassie just picked up her gym bag and sauntered out to her Fiat without a backward glance.

"So who'd you pick?" Richmond asked me as I gathered up my stuff.

"I'm not about to tell you before I tell her," I said, pulling a sweatshirt on over my leotard.

"How'd it go, Amber-Lynn?" Crater asked when Richmond and I reached the front of the gym.

I hated that Crater called me Amber-Lynn instead of just Amber. It's so country. That's something else he and my momma have in common.

"It went fine," I told Crater. "We'll be in to rehearse Saturday at noon, okay?"

"Anything you want is okay by me!" Crater agreed enthusiastically.

"That ole boy's got a crush on you," Richmond teased as we walked out to his car.

"So do lots of guys," I told him with a smile.

"You are bad!" Richmond exclaimed. He tried to swat my butt, but I dodged away from his hand.

On the way to my house, Richmond chattered about the tryouts for the football team, but I didn't pay him much mind. I was too busy thinking about Sizzle and all my plans for the future.

"Can I come in?" Richmond asked hopefully when he pulled up in front of my house.

"No, you cannot," I told him, but I leaned close and gave him a hot kiss right after I said it.

"You make me crazy," Richmond murmured.

"I know that, Richie," I said huskily, and kissed him again. Then I hopped out of his car.

"I'll call you later, sweet thing!" he called to me.

I waved behind my back and walked to the front door.

"I'm home," I called, and the screen door banged shut behind me.

There was no answer, just a note from Momma that she'd gone to the store with our neighbor, Kayla Gaines, who had a car that, unlike *our* car, actually worked.

I dropped my books on the table and looked around the room. Pages from a movie magazine were glued to the wall to cover a large crack that ran from ceiling to floor. The kitchen table was an old door propped up on cinderblocks. A dirty oil cloth covered part of the counter, on it the grotty pieces of our black-and-white TV, which one of Momma's gentlemen callers said he would fix. There was nothing fine or lovely anywhere I looked.

Of course I hadn't invited Richmond in. I never

had, and I never would. Just having him see the front of my house was bad enough, but at least I had planted some flowers and painted the shutters light blue, and that helped. Inside, though, was much, much worse.

No one who counted was ever going to see inside.

CHAPTER TWO

"Amber-Lynn, baby, come help me with these groceries!"

It was about an hour later, and I was doing my history homework in the one and only bedroom. I put my history book down on the bed and sighed. Momma was perfectly capable of putting away the groceries herself. After all, on our budget, how much could she have possibly bought?

"Look who's here, baby!" Momma cried festively when I padded barefoot into the kitchen.

"Gee, it's Kyle. What a surprise," I said sarcastically as I reached for the milk to put it in the refrigerator.

Kyle Gaines is Kayla's son. They live two doors down from us. Because Kayla and Momma were best friends, they were always trying to throw me and Kyle at each other. Kyle is a year older than me, and by pure coincidence he is also on scholarship at Covington. Well, I guess it isn't exactly pure coincidence. It's because Kyle got in on a scholarship when he was in the seventh grade that Kayla and Momma came up with this idea of my applying, too.

"Where do you want the canned goods, Miz Harkin?" Kyle asked Momma, completely ignoring me.

"Just on the counter is fine," Momma told him. "I got that creamed corn you like so much on sale, four for a dollar just because the cans were a little dented!" she added for my benefit.

Excruciating.

"So did ya'll see each other at school today?" Momma coaxed, refusing to let it go.

"I really didn't notice," I said coolly.

"Well, gee, I saw you, Amber," Kyle said, leaning against the oil cloth on the counter. "You had on a new outfit to impress ole Rich Richie Remington."

"His name is Richmond," I snapped. It was one thing for me to call him Richie, and quite another for Kyle.

"Well, I stand corrected," Kyle said gravely.

I looked over at him, standing there in his faded jeans and T-shirt, which I had to admit he filled out to perfection, and I wanted to wipe the smirk off his handsome face with a big fat smack.

Kyle's turning out handsome had sort of snuck up on me. I mean, I'd known him my whole life, and he was always kind of runty and funny-looking with big ears. Then it seemed like overnight his head grew and his ears didn't, and he got tall and muscular, and just like that he was a hunk. Of course, I still hated him. He knew entirely too much about me, and vice versa.

I ignored Kyle when he said good-bye, and helped Momma put away the last of the groceries. As usual, she made a mess as she worked, leaving the bags out on the counter and spilling a trail of milk from the leaking carton.

"How about some creamed corn for supper?" Momma asked. "I could cook up some greens, or maybe some soup . . ."

I knew what she was trying to do—distract me from the question she knew I was going to ask anyway.

"Where were you last night?" I asked, grabbing a sponge and wiping up the spilled milk.

"Or how about spaghetti!" she continued. "I'm in the mood for noodles, myself."

"I asked where you were last night," I repeated, folding the paper bags and sticking them behind the refrigerator.

"I got in late is all," Momma said. She grabbed the sponge and nervously wiped off the counter, which no amount of sponging would ever actually clean. That's when I knew for sure she was lying—Momma only cleans when she feels guilty.

"You didn't get in at all," I corrected.

"I was fast asleep right there when you went off to school," she defended herself, pointing to the pull-out bed in the living room that still sat open and disheveled.

"I heard you sneak in when it was already dawn," I told her. I knew her waitress shift at the Brass Rail, this tacky tourist trap on Printer's Alley, ended at 2 A.M.

"Oh, I just met up with a friend," she said finally, "just being social."

I faced her with my hands on my hips. "His initials wouldn't be J.J., would they?" I asked her.

"Now, Amber," Momma began, "J.J. is a very decent man. You've no call to—"

"Momma!" I interrupted her. "You promised!"

Jeremy James—or J.J., as everyone called him—was Momma's great weakness in life. He was a long-distance trucker who zoomed in and out of her life. When he was sober, he was even a decent guy. Trouble was, he wasn't often sober.

In between each of J.J.'s many departures and arrivals, Momma went out with what she referred to as her "gentlemen callers." Usually they were tourists she met at the club, and they lasted only a night or two. Momma made sure they picked her up proper at her front door, and they returned her home at the end of their date. What she did in between was something I couldn't stand to think about. Growing up with all these gentlemen callers hanging around is the main reason I'm still a virgin. I am so much smarter than my mother.

See, Momma had me when she was only sixteen years old. She doesn't know exactly who my daddy was, since he could have been one of several. I've seen old pictures of Momma, and she looked a lot like me. But that's all she thought she had going for her.

So from the time she was thirteen and got a figure, she fell in love with just about every boy who paid attention to her. And she thought that if you were in love, it was okay to share your love in a physical way. I guess with all that sharing it's a wonder she didn't get pregnant even sooner.

Sometimes I look at Momma, and if I squint real hard, I see how she could be, instead of how she is. Her bad bleach job and home perm are transformed into something soft and flattering. The frosted blue eyeshadow and gloppy lip gloss is replaced with something subtle and tasteful. She has on white linen trousers instead of those too-tight jeans she always wears, and her cleavage is for once left to the imagination. She would look beautiful.

"I know I promised I wouldn't see him no more, Amber," Momma said, "but that was only on account of the drinking. He was sober as a judge, and he was very nice to me."

It was pathetic. Momma lived on the hope that one day J.J. would ask her to marry him and they'd go trucking off into the sunset. Then when he went on a bender and hit her, or just didn't show up for weeks or months at a time, she'd swear she was through with him. Then she'd fall in love with someone new about once or twice a week. Momma is in love with love.

"Fine," I snapped at her. "Do what you want."

"Let's don't fight, sweet pea," Momma said, pushing some hair off my face. I shook her hand away. "How were your auditions?"

"I think we found the right girl," I told her. "Her name is Cassie Stewart."

"Did you tell her yet?" Momma asked, opening a can of corn.

"I'm going to call her after dinner," I said, getting out a saucepan.

"Why make her wait like that?" Momma asked. "I bet she's dying to hear."

"That's just the point," I explained patiently. "The longer she has to wait, the more insecure she'll feel."

"Well, why would you want to put her through all that?" Momma wanted to know.

"It's psychological warfare," I answered. Momma looked perplexed. "Forget it. You wouldn't understand. I'm going to go finish my homework. Call me when dinner's ready."

I waited to call Cassie until after I finished

dinner and did all my homework. Then around nine thirty, I dialed her number.

"Stewart residence," came a well-modulated voice over the phone.

"Is Cassie in?" I asked.

"You can reach Cassandra on her private line," the voice said, and gave me another number before hanging up.

I looked down at the three-by-five card on which Cassie had written her information, and sure enough, there were two phone numbers. Of course she had her own phone. I dialed the other number, and Cassie picked up on the third ring.

"Yes?" she said, cool as you please.

"Cassie, this is Amber," I said, equally cool.

"Yes?" she asked, as if she couldn't care less why I might be phoning her.

"I'm calling to offer you the opening with Sizzle," I said.

"Great!" This time she couldn't keep the enthusiasm out of her voice.

"Of course, it's conditional," I continued. "Say for the first three months. I have to make sure you're good enough."

I knew she wanted to call me names, to tell me

where to go, but she wanted to be in Sizzle even more, so she struggled to be civil. "That's fine," she assured me.

Before I hung up, I told her our rehearsal schedule and that our first gig was already booked for the Ace of Clubs—this very happening local club—in two weeks. It was very important that Cassie Stewart know exactly who was boss.

As long as I kept Cassie in line, I thought that with her as the third dancer, Sizzle would be even better than it had been before. I lay down on my bed, staring up at the cracked ceiling, visions of fame and fortune whirling through my mind. Because I knew, as surely as I knew that J.J. would get drunk again or that Momma would fall in love with some crude, dumb tourist who would never love her back, that dancing was my ticket out of there.

"Amber, baby, you know I love you," Richmond groaned in my ear.

It was Friday night, and Richmond and I had gone to see some stupid movie where buildings kept blowing up and cars kept crashing. It seemed like most any other night—the usual wrestling session between me and Richmond, him trying to get all over me, me diverting his attention. It's funny how sometimes the big milestones of your life sneak right by, and you don't appreciate them until later.

Anyway, after we wrestled all during the movie, we drove out past Smyrna and parked at the end of a deserted, dead-end road to wrestle some more.

"You're sweet, Richie," I whispered back, running my hands fetchingly down his muscular chest.

Richmond took that for a positive sign. As he kissed me passionately, his right hand headed south under my white cotton miniskirt. I pulled his hand out per usual, and continued to kiss him.

"I can't take much more of this," he moaned.

"Poor baby," I cooed.

"Everyone at school thinks we're doing it," Richmond pleaded, "so what difference does it make?"

I sat up and pushed him away. "What kind of logic is that?" I asked him.

"I just meant—" he began.

"Did you tell anyone we were doing it?" I demanded.

"No," he answered quickly, "it's just that a girl who comes on as hot as you do . . ." He let the rest of his sentence dangle in the air.

"What?" I snapped. "I must be cheap?"

"No, I didn't mean that at all—" Richmond said with frustration. He hit his hand hard on the steering wheel. Finally he looked at me. "Doesn't the fact that I love you mean anything to you?"

"Of course it does," I said in a soft voice, snuggling close to him. "But I'm just not ready." I rained soft little kisses on his neck until I felt him give in. He put his arms around me and kissed me on the lips. "When I'm ready, it'll be you," I lied.

"I hope it's some time before I'm middle-aged," he grumbled, starting up his car and heading back to my house.

"Can I come in?" he asked when we arrived. He always asked.

"I'm sure my mother's asleep," I told him. Of course that was a total lie. I knew perfectly well Momma was at the Brass Rail. I had told Richmond and all the rest of the kids at school that my mother was a nurse at Vanderbilt Medical Center, and my daddy—who had been a surgeon— had died in a terrible car wreck when I was a baby. That explained why my mother and I now lived in genteel poverty. I kissed Richmond passionately and got out of his car.

"Amber, wait!" he said, scooting over to call to me out of the window of the passenger side of the car.

"Shhhh! It's late!" I admonished him, as if I lived in a decent neighborhood where folks could get upset by a late night voice.

"How come when I tell you I love you, you never say it back?" Richmond whispered into the night air.

I walked back over to the car and leaned down. "When I say it—*if* I say it, Richie, you'll know I really mean it."

"I'll be waiting for that day, Amber," Richmond said.

"I know you will," I told him tenderly, tracing the outline of his lips with my finger. " 'Night."

CHAPTER THREE

You know that feeling where you're not stay-in-bed sick, but you feel just rotten enough to treat everyone around you like dirt? That's how I woke up feeling the next morning.

It was Saturday, the day of Sizzle's first rehearsal with Cassie, and I knew it would set the tone for everything. I felt kind of achy all over, but no way was I going to miss this practice.

"Hi, baby. Don't you look sharp," Momma said when I came out of my bedroom in my warm-up clothes. She was standing in front of the cracked mirror on the dresser, waving a caked mascara wand over her eyelashes.

"Where are you going?" I asked her, taking in her too-tight, too-short, too-low-cut flowery dress.

"That sweetheart J.J. is taking me on a picnic," she exclaimed girlishly, adding another coat of mascara.

"What's on the menu, besides beer?" I asked, pouring myself a cup of coffee.

"Now, Amber, it isn't like that this time," Momma assured me. She sat down on the daybed and looked at me expectantly. "I think this might really be it."

"Be what?" I asked her.

"I think he's finally ready to pop the question," she said.

"The only thing J.J. is ready to pop is your face," I said. I walked to the front door and looked out for Donna, who was picking me up for rehearsal any minute.

"You're very hard for a young girl," Momma said, gathering up her dignity and her purse at the same time.

I didn't respond to that. Why bother?

"You should eat a little breakfast before you go," Momma urged me gently. "You can't dance on an empty stomach, baby." She went to the cupboard and took out the Frosted Flakes. "Have some cereal."

"Donna's here," I said, when I saw her Jeep

pull up in front of the house. "Bye, Momma." I picked up my gym bag, kissed Momma's cheek, and flew out the front door.

"Hi," Donna said, when I got into her Jeep. She turned it around and headed back towards town. "I have to tell you, I do not have a good feeling about Cassie Stewart."

"Donna, you've told me that every day since I picked her, so give it a rest," I snapped.

"Okay, okay," Donna sighed. "But don't say I didn't warn you. I just think she's trouble, is all."

"Look, I can handle Cassie Stewart," I told her, gathering my hair in a ponytail so the wind wouldn't whip it in my face. "How about if you just worry about keeping up yourself."

Donna made a sound in the back of her throat. "Oh, well, excuse me for having an opinion." We drove the rest of the way in silence.

"Hey, Amber-Lynn!" Crater cried when he saw me walk in. "Long time no see!"

That was Crater's idea of a joke. I had seen him just the day before, when I taught an advanced aerobics class right after school.

Cassie was already waiting for us in the back dance studio. I certainly couldn't fault her for punctuality. She was at the barre, doing warm-up stretches.

"Make sure you do your warm-ups before rehearsal," I told her, setting the cassette player on the table. "We don't take up rehearsal time with that."

Cassie raised her eyebrows at me. "I was just finishing," she said regally.

"Good," I told her, going through the tapes. "Let's start with 'Buff Enough,' since you learned part of it for the audition already." I stuck the cassette into the player. "Watch Donna and I do the whole routine, and then we'll break it down," I told her. Cassie nodded and sat exquisitely cross-legged by the mirrored wall.

Donna and I danced full-out to the blaring funk tune, legs kicking, arms flying. On the final chorus I threw my arms up, did the double pirouette going into the hip-hop section, then scissored my arms down double-time.

That was when I felt that pain again, a sharp stab in my right wrist. I ignored it and concentrated on the music, diving into the one-handed push-ups that finished the routine.

But my wrist wouldn't hold me. On the second

push-up my wrist collapsed. Donna held the final pose, breathing hard, looking at me in the mirror laying there on my stomach.

"What happened?" she asked me.

"I think I sprained my wrist or something," I said, rotating it gingerly.

"I've got an Ace bandage in my gym bag," Cassie offered, rummaging through her stuff.

"It's no big thing. Just forget it," I said. I wasn't taking any charity from *her*. I got up and walked over to the cassette player and pressed rewind.

We worked on "Buff Enough" for the next hour, arms, legs, and sweat flying through the air. Cassie was picking up the routine quickly—much more quickly than Donna had, in fact. I drove her relentlessly anyway.

"No, it's a double hip-roll into the release, Cassie. I just told you that!" I barked when she missed a difficult syncopated section for the second time.

"Sorry," she mumbled.

"Don't be sorry, be right," I snapped, and we did it again.

It was very irritating not to be able to do the

one-handed push-ups at the end of the routine, which just added to my horrid mood.

"Hey, let's take a break," Donna panted after an hour and a half.

"I don't need a break," I said. I looked over at Cassie. "Do you?" I challenged her.

"No," she said, staring me down.

"Well, good, you're both Superwoman, but I've got to pee and get some water," Donna said huffily, and she stalked off to the ladies' room.

Cassie ignored me and faced the mirror. Counting off in her head, she went over the double hip-roll section she had messed up, and did it perfectly. Twice.

"Better," I said grudgingly when she walked over to me.

"I know," she replied snottily, wiping off her neck with her hand towel. "Your choreography is really good, you know," she added.

Now it was my turn to be snotty. "I know," I said.

"Okay, I'm a new woman," Donna said cheerfully when she walked back into the studio.

We took "Buff Enough" from the top, and we were sensational. Maybe it was just the adrenaline, but my right wrist felt fine and supported me perfectly during the one-handed push-ups. We finished in position, each with one leg crossed over the other's, our hands straight up in the air.

"Oo-wee!" Crater cheered from the doorway, clapping his hands and whistling through his teeth. "That was better than the Dallas Cowgirls, no lie! It was even better than *Star Search*!"

Star Search. It was like a light bulb going on in my head. Why hadn't I thought of it before? Maybe because with Missy we weren't nearly as good as we were with Cassie. But now I could see the potential after just one rehearsal. Cassie was really, really good. And Sizzle should compete on *Star Search*. No. Sizzle should *win Star Search*.

"Hey, I'll fetch ya'll some of that Perrier from the fridge," Crater offered, disappearing from the doorway.

"Ya'll, I've just made a decision," I said, sitting cross-legged on the floor. My wrist was starting to ache again, and I rubbed it absentmindedly.

"I assume you're going to share it with us," Cassie said, wiping her neck with her monogrammed towel.

"Soon, very soon, Sizzle is goin' to be too big for Nashville," I said contemplatively.

"Well, my mother won't let me go to Memphis, not even to see Graceland," Donna said.

I shot her a look of pure disgust. "I'm not talkin' about *Memphis,* Donna," I said scornfully. "I'm talking about *TV.*"

"TV?" Donna echoed breathlessly.

Cassie just stared at me, waiting.

"I'm talkin' about *Star Search,*" I said. "We're going to kick butt until we're perfect, and then we're going to make a videotape to submit to *Star Search.*"

"Awesome!" Donna screeched. "That would be absolutely awesome!"

"I think we should vote on it," Cassie said. "It should be a three-way decision."

I stood up and flicked my hair back over my shoulders. "Maybe you need to be reminded that you're still on probation," I replied, "which would make it a two-way decision—if we were going to vote, that is. But we're not."

Cassie took a step towards me and stared me in the eye. "The only reason you're thinking about *Star Search* now is because you know that Sizzle is much better with me in it."

"You got something against success?" I asked her, ignoring her comment completely. "Because if you do, you better say so now."

She stared at me a moment, and I stared right back. "*Star Search* is a good idea," she said finally, turning away.

"Here's your drinks, ladies," Crater called, eagerly handing over the cold green bottles. "Dang if I don't have me three stars right back here in the dance studio!"

"Thanks, Crater," I said, tossing back the Perrier. I looked at my watch. "Drink up, we're moving on to 'Burning Love.'"

Donna always had a little trouble with "Burning Love," one of the last tunes we'd added before Missy left the group. I told Donna to sit with Cassie and watch, and I went through the whole routine by myself. Was it my imagination, or did my legs feel weaker than usual? I was so out of breath when I finished the number that I had to turn away from Donna and Cassie so they wouldn't see how much I was panting.

"Hot momma!" I heard from the doorway, and there was Richie, grinning at me. "Girl, you are poetry in motion."

"Thanks," I said, breathing hard. I walked

over to the doorway. "What are you doing here?"

"Enjoying the view," he said, still grinning.

"Well, we're trying to work, so you'll have to go enjoy some other view," I snapped. It's not that I was really so annoyed at Richmond. I was annoyed at myself for being so out of breath from one little dance number.

"Hey, Richmond," Cassie said, sauntering over to the doorway.

He gave her his boyish grin and took in how cute she looked in her sexy dance clothes. "Hey, Cassie. How's it going?"

"You'd have to ask sarge here," Cassie said, cocking her head in my direction. "I'm just a dancing fool."

"How about if we do 'Buff Enough' for Richmond?" Donna suggested eagerly.

"We're not putting on a show," I barked, "we're rehearsing."

"Oh, come on, sweetheart," Richmond urged. "Don't be that way."

"Right," Cassie echoed in her slightly mocking voice. "Don't be that way." She took a step closer to Richmond and looked up at him from under her long, long eyelashes. "I'd love to show you."

"Fine," I allowed, "but this doesn't count as

rehearsal time. Which means we're working late to make up the difference." I marched over to the cassette player and stuck in "Buff Enough," then I took my position.

Damn, we looked good. My mind was whirling at a thousand miles an hour. This would be the number we'd tape for *Star Search*. Turn, turn, bump, head-roll, isolation. Down into the really gymnastic part, which was all the more impressive because it came at the end, when a mere mortal would be tired. Not us. I could see in the mirror that Donna and Cassie were right with me, dropping to the one-handed push ups, full-out, and into the big finish. No problems for me. My wrist felt fine; my energy was there; I was a star.

"Unbelievable!" Richmond whooped. "I can't believe ya'll just started working together!"

"We're gonna be on *Star Search*!" Donna yelled with excitement.

"Say, now!" Richmond commented, obviously surprised.

Donna never knew when to keep her mouth shut. Having her blurt that information out to Richmond was not my plan at all. In fact, Richmond—or to put it more bluntly, Richmond's money—was part of my plan to actually get on

Star Search. He would pay for us to make a really professional video. All I had to do was to convince him of the wisdom of such an investment.

"Donna, put in 'Burning Love,' and you two work on it. I'll be right back." I took Richmond by the arm and walked with him into the hall.

"Suddenly you've got time for me?" he asked.

"I always have time for you," I cooed, rubbing up against him.

"You're a big tease, Amber," he said, but I could tell that the feel of my lithe body up against him was burning off the mad he was hankering for.

"Well, even when I don't have time for you, I'm thinking about you," I said with a demure smile.

"Oh, yeah? What are you thinking?"

"Evil things," I breathed and kissed him softly on the lips. Then I took a step back and threw back my head, blotting the towel at the low neckline of my leotard. "I'm hot."

"What time you finishing?" he asked, mesmerized by the good fortune of that towel, now sliding in between my breasts.

"In about an hour," I said casually. "So, what do you think of this *Star Search* idea?"

"I think it's great," he said, still eyeing the towel.

"What we need to do is to send in a video," I continued, "a really professional video."

"That sounds about right," he agreed.

I moved towards him again. "It costs some money to do a really professional video," I said. "And I think you should be our sponsor."

He laughed. "You do, do you?"

"I do," I said. I put my arms around his neck and stared into his eyes. "Will you do it for me?"

"Depends," he said, his eyes narrowing. "What are you going to do for me?"

"Everything," I promised in a low voice.

"Everything?" he echoed, his voice cracking a little.

"Well, Richie, if you were to do this little thing for me, I'd know that you really respected my career," I said. "And that means a lot."

"Uh huh," he grunted. As thoughts of "everything" danced in his head, his IQ was slumping rapidly.

"So does that mean you'll sponsor Sizzle, pay for our video?" I pressed.

"Uh huh," he repeated.

"Good." I kissed him a kiss full of promise,

waved good-bye, and walked back into rehearsal. I was going to find out who the best video guy in Nashville was, and Richie Rich was going to pay for it. Sizzle was on its way to *Star Search*.

As far as "everything" went, I of course meant to keep my promise.

Just not necessarily in this lifetime.

CHAPTER FOUR

"Remind me again why I bought this thing," Donna said, morosely staring at her reflection in the mirror.

"Because it is so hot," I said, turning over on her bed and popping the last cashew into my mouth. I hadn't had much of an appetite lately—even my jeans seemed to be getting looser—so I was relishing my newfound hunger.

"Well, I look like death warmed over. Black is definitely not my color."

She was right. The black minidress she had on was cute, all right—the whole middle from just under her breasts down to her hip bones was made of see-through mesh—but with her olive coloring and dark hair she looked just awful in it. Of course, I had known that would be the case the instant I'd picked the dress out and urged Donna to try it on. And I'd certainly known it when I told her how sexy that dress was as she posed in the dressing room. Being bright enough to trust in my good taste, she'd bought it on a whim—along with a few other cute things she just couldn't live without.

But as awful as I knew that dress looked on Donna, is how good I knew it would look on me.

Which was the whole point.

"Try on the red suede shirt with the fringe," I suggested casually, as Donna threw the expensive new black dress on the bed.

"Try the black dress on if you want," Donna said, fumbling through her huge overstuffed shopping bags to find the new red shirt. "You can have it if it fits."

Bingo.

I knew she would offer me that dress as surely as I knew she would be too lazy to return it. Donna is filthy rich and has absolutely no sense about money.

The way I figured it, I deserved a new dress, and God knows I'd never be able to afford one. It was, after all, my birthday party we were getting dressed for, and I wasn't about to wear just any old outfit. Not only was I celebrating my sixteenth birthday, but at the party (which was being held at The Gym, compliments of Crater) we were all going to see the video premier of Sizzle dancing to "Buff Enough," which had been made two days earlier. The very next day I planned to mail it off to *Star Search*. I had to look like the star I was about to become.

It hadn't been easy, either, getting ready for that video. Donna, Cassie, and I had been working really hard, rehearsing nearly every day after school, and on the weekends, too. Between that, cheerleader practice, school, and teaching aerobics, I was exhausted. At least, that's why I thought I was exhausted. Sometimes in the mornings my whole body seemed to feel stiff until I'd stood under a steaming hot shower for five minutes. Other times only a certain joint would hurt, particularly after rehearsal. Frankly, it annoyed the hell out of me. My body had never failed me, and I just assumed it never would.

What a laugh.

"My black leather miniskirt with this, don't you think?" Donna asked, snapping my mind back to the present.

"Right," I agreed. I got up, slipped the black

dress over my head, and turned to Donna. "Well?"

"Oh, you'd look hot in a paper bag," Donna muttered, not bothering to look at me. She buttoned up her new red suede-and-leather shirt, which cost more than my entire wardrobe, and eyed herself critically in the mirror. "With red lipstick, do you think? Or would that be tacky?"

"Definitely red lipstick," I told her. I sat back down on her bed and spilled my cosmetics out of my purse. When a natural blonde wears black, she needs a little extra color.

"Oh, hey, I forgot to tell you!" Donna screeched, spinning around from her mirror. "You will not believe who's bringing Bitsy Renfrey to your party tonight."

"Billy Ray Cyrus?" I suggested, swiping my blush brush across my cheeks.

"In her dreams," Donna scoffed. "No, it's Kyle Gaines!"

"*My* Kyle Gaines?" I replied before I could stop myself.

Donna raised her eyebrows at me, thinking maybe she was getting some dirt that she hadn't previously known. Donna lives for dirt, most of which she makes up herself, passes on, and then believes by the time it comes back around to her.

"You can get your eyebrows out of your hair line," I told her. "All I meant was the Kyle Gaines I know."

"Were you two an item before you came to Covington?" Donna asked eagerly. "He is to die for."

"Trust me, we never were an item, and we will never be an item," I said tersely, putting an extra coat of mascara on my eyelashes.

"I don't see why not," Donna said. "He's totally fine."

"He is a complete hick from the sticks, is what he is," I replied testily. "What's he doing going out with Bitsy Renfrey, anyway?"

"I have no idea," Donna said. "I mean, he writes for the literary magazine and so does she, so I guess that's how they know each other. But a date? There's just no accounting for taste, is there?"

"Excuse me, Miss Donna," the housekeeper said politely from the doorway. "This here is a package just dropped off for Amber."

I really wanted to correct her, and say "Miss Amber to you," but I couldn't. The reason was that the Martin family's housekeeper was Celine

Booth, the older sister of Winnella Booth, who was my best friend before I transferred to Covington and got an actual life.

"Thanks," I said, taking the package from Celine. I thought about adding "say hey to Winnella for me," but the look she shot me was so hateful that I kept my mouth shut. Anyway, why blow my cover for her? Donna, of course, had no clue that I'd once been in the same circle as her housekeeper.

"What could this be?" I mused, as I opened the little card on top of the gaily wrapped box.

"I remember you once admired this in a magazine," I read out loud, "and I knew it would look even prettier on you. Happy birthday from your friend forever, Crater."

"From Crater! How'd he even know you were here?"

"He asked me yesterday where I'd be before the party, and I told him I'd be getting ready at your house," I said, as I tore the paper off the box. Inside, nestled in thin pink tissue paper were many, many Swatch watches, each one different from the others.

"There must be a dozen watches in there!" Donna exclaimed, hovering over the box. "That's totally cool, but it's the weirdest present I ever saw!"

"No, it's not," I said. I pulled out the page Crater had torn from a fashion magazine and laid under the watches. There was a picture of a model with gorgeous, long, thick hair. And tying back her hair were a dozen brightly colored Swatch watches, each fastened on a tighter notch as they paraded down her hair. One day when I'd been at The Gym flipping through a magazine I'd seen that ad, and I'd remarked to Crater how wonderful I thought it looked. I guess Crater remembered.

Donna helped me fasten the watches in my hair, then I stood with my back to her full-length mirror and twisted around to see my hair. It looked awesome.

"You realize that I hate you for having perfect hair," Donna sighed, staring at me glumly.

"You can't hate me; it's my birthday," I replied. "Hey, what time is it, anyway?"

"Amber, you are wearing twelve watches in your hair!"

"Well, I didn't set them!" I exclaimed, catching a glimpse of the time on the clock on Donna's dresser.

"Excuse me, Miss Donna," Celine said, once

again appearing at the door. "Mr. Richmond is downstairs."

"Let's boogie!" Donna cried, picking up her purse.

"Don't hurry, Donna," I chastised her. "Never hurry for a guy."

Donna put her hands on her hips. "What am I supposed to do, stand here and pretend we're still getting dressed?"

"You could sit," I suggested.

Donna sighed deeply and sat down next to me. "How long do we have to sit here?"

"Oh, say . . . long enough to sing 'The Star Spangled Banner,' " I decided.

"How many verses?" Donna asked sarcastically.

I laughed, and felt the Swatch watches tickling down my back. "Why, Donna, you made an actual joke. That's progress!"

"Somehow your compliments never really sound like compliments," Donna grumbled.

"O'er the land of the free! And the home of . . . the . . . brave!" I sang lustily. "That should just about do it." I picked up my purse and slung the strap over my shoulder, then I turned to Donna. "Coming?"

Donna rolled her eyes, but of course she followed me out of her room.

"Hey, Richmond!" Donna called gaily when we reached her huge marble front hall.

"Hey, yourself," he answered, but his eyes were glued to me in my new black mesh minidress and my Swatch-adorned hair. "I could get arrested just for lookin' at you," he told me.

"Not unless I press charges," I replied, standing on tip-toe to brush a kiss against his lips.

"I've got a surprise for you, birthday girl," Richmond murmured, grinning at me.

"Now what would that be?" I asked, but as soon as we stepped out the door, I knew. There stood a long, white stretch limousine with a uniformed driver standing at the door.

"You sweetheart!" I cried, throwing my arms around Richmond's neck.

"Get your fine *be*-hind into this car!" Bobby Pratt called, sticking his head out the back window. "We're ready to pop the champagne—compliments of my father's secret stash," Bobby announced. "Just do me a favor and don't tell him I stole it!"

When the chauffeur helped Donna and Richie and me into the car, there were six of our friends, already crowded in. Bobby Pratt, who sometimes went out with Donna, and Misty Salinger, Lindsey Van Owen, Cassie Stewart, Chase Monroe, and Spencer Hayden. They were easily the coolest, richest kids at school.

"Here's to Amber!" Richmond announced, clinking his glass against everyone else's.

"Remember us little people when you get famous!" Bobby announced, sipping at his champagne.

"Please, I've forgotten you already!" I replied.

"Your hair is so unbelievable," Misty said, making me sit forward so she could see all the Swatch watches. "I didn't know you had all those watches."

"I didn't," I said. "They were a birthday present."

"From who?" Richmond asked, a frown on his face.

"Someone who lusts after me," I teased.

"Shoot, Amber, that's every guy I know!" Richmond grumbled.

"Poor puppy," I cooed, and laughed at the anguish on his face. I sat back against the cool white leather upholstery, then relented and leaned forward to kiss Richmond. I intended for it to be a sweet little thank-you kiss, but he held me close and made it into something much bigger. So I kissed him back, making sure everyone could see just how I did it (especially Cassie) until the boys were hooting and hollering at us.

"We need to hose these two down!" Chase yelped.

I pulled away from Richie and smiled at all my friends. I felt great.

I was having so much fun in that limo that I told the driver to drive around for a while. I wished Momma and Kyle and everyone from my neighborhood could see me, sitting there sipping fine French champagne in the back of a white stretch limousine.

By the time we got to The Gym, the party was already in full swing. Crater's face lit up when he saw me. I spun around in a circle, so he could see all those watches in my hair.

"It looks even better than I figured," Crater said shyly, grinning from ear to ear.

"I think it's a wonderful present," I told him, and kissed him on the cheek. "You're the sweetest."

"You deserve beautiful things, Amber-Lynn," Crater said earnestly.

"Come on and dance with me," Richmond called, pulling on my arm.

I whirled into the middle of the floor and gave myself over to the music. Richmond and I danced until he got thirsty and went off in search of something to drink.

"Happy birthday," a deep male voice said from behind me.

I turned around. It was Kyle. He had on jeans and a T-shirt with a picture of John Lennon on it, and he looked extremely fine.

"Thanks," I said in a flat voice, lifting my hair to fan the back of my neck.

"I'll bet there's a real good reason you've got a dozen watches in your hair," Kyle mused, "but I'll be hog-tied to a tadpole if I can think of what it is."

I dropped my hair and gave him an evil look. He only used those stupid hick expressions to get my goat. "It's called fashion," I snapped, "a subject about which you have no knowledge at all."

"That's true," Kyle agreed. "I mean, from my point of view it just seems like conspicuous consumption, but then I guess I'm just ignorant."

"Do you think that just because your head finally swelled up enough to support those big ole ears of yours that you can be nasty to me?" I asked him.

"Nope, I always thought I could be nasty to you," Kyle replied. "It's just that I didn't used to want to be."

"Here's your Coke, Kyle," Bitsy said, sidling up to Kyle and handing him the cold can. She took his arm and held it proprietarily against her side. Even though I had talked myself into believing I didn't give a hoot who Kyle went out with, it still galled me to see him with another girl. I suppose deep in my heart I had always believed that one day it would be him and me. But I would have swallowed nails before I let him—or anyone else—know the truth.

"Hey, Bitsy, don't you look precious," I told her. She had on a flowered dress with a drop waist that pulled across her thighs and made her look like a festively decorated sack of potatos.

"Thanks," Bitsy said, blushing happily and pulling even more tightly on Kyle's arm. "Happy birthday."

"Aren't you sweet," I said, giving her my sugariest smile. "And aren't the two of you just the most darlingest couple?"

"Oh, well, it's only our first date," Bitsy said,

blushing even more furiously and increasing her death-grip on Kyle's arm.

"Do tell!" I marveled.

"We both write for *The Bard*," she explained eagerly, naming Covington's literary magazine.

"Well, Bitsy, honey," I drawled, "I don't think Kyle's gonna get much writing done with his arm all mashed up against your bosom like that! You could ruin his circulation for life!"

"Oh!" Bitsy cried in embarrassment, and she dropped Kyle's arm like it had caught fire.

"It's okay, Bits," Kyle said quietly. "Let's dance." Then he took Bitsy in his arms and turned away from me completely.

You may be wondering why I was so hateful to Kyle.

Back when we were friends—a really long time ago—we used to tell each other everything. Kyle's big dream was to be a songwriter. His momma got him an old guitar at a pawn shop, and he taught himself to play. We even started making up songs together. We used to hang out at the creek behind my house for hours, sitting on the hood of our old Ford without an engine, singing songs we'd make up together. It was our special place, where no one else would go. I'd talk about how one day I'd be this famous dancer, and Kyle would talk about how Reba McEntire or Ricky Van Shelton or even Willie Nelson would sing his songs, and we'd live in a mansion out on Franklin Road with a swimming pool in the shape of a guitar in the back. I believed him. Frankly, I thought he'd hung the moon, and I didn't care anything about his stupid big ears.

Because, see, having Kyle as my best friend made everything okay. Our house didn't seem so bad, and going to school every day where Dee-Dee Derky beat me up in the playground out of sheer meanness didn't seem so bad, and even Momma and her gentlemen callers didn't seem so bad.

Until this one time. I was twelve, and I was asleep on the pull-out bed in the living room when Momma and her latest gentleman caller came in. He was drunk and he asked Momma for coffee. We didn't have any coffee, but Momma was so eager to please that she said she'd pop on over to Kayla Gaines's house and borrow some—she knew Kyle's mom was an insomniac who stayed up all night watching old movies on TV.

When Momma left I kept my eyes closed, pretending to be asleep, and I felt the bed go lower as the man sat down next to me. I concentrated on breathing real regularly so he wouldn't see that I was afraid. But then I could feel his breath on me, and I smelled that sickening smell of stale liquor, and my eyes popped open on their own. I stared at him, waiting.

Without saying a word, he put his huge, ugly hand on my T-shirt right over my newly grown breasts. I jumped and he jumped, and the next thing I knew he was on top of me and I was fighting and screaming, but he was big and drunk and ugly, and then Kyle came running in that front door, and even though he was a skinny kid with big ears he pulled that bastard off of me.

Then Momma came running back in, and when she saw what had happened she threw the jar of Maxwell House Instant at the man and got him good, right on the forehead. Momma was crying and Kyle was screaming about how could she leave me alone like that—she was an unfit mother and a whoring tramp. I couldn't stand that. I screamed at Kyle to get the hell out of our house and never come back.

I knew as soon as he walked out the door that I was screaming at the wrong person, but I was too busy comforting Momma to go after him.

The next day the scene kept playing itself out in my head—Kyle had seen practically everything—and I was too embarrassed to apologize to him.

A few days after that I got my first boyfriend, Lionel Pritcher, and we were soul-kissing sitting on the old Ford by the creek when Kyle came along with his guitar. He took one look at Lionel and me sucking face in that spot that was supposed to be our private place, and he called me a little tramp-slut-whore with no morals who would grow up to be just like my whoring momma, and then he ran away.

I never spoke to him again in a civil way.

"Hey, ya'll, it's show time!" Richmond yelled, and I tore my eyes away from Kyle and Bitsy Renfrey dancing close to a slow song. We all gathered around the huge TV Crater had set up, and Richmond popped the Sizzle video into the VCR.

The pounding beat of "Buff Enough" filled the air, and there we were, dancing perfectly to my choreography. I tried to look at it objectively, to compare how good we were to how good the dance acts on *Star Search* were.

We were better.

When the tape ended everyone applauded and

screamed and whistled. I looked over at Donna and Cassie, who were beaming with happiness and excitement. All my friends came over and started hugging and kissing me, and telling me how wonderful I was, how talented, how terrific, how fabulous.

I certainly didn't need a low-down liar like Kyle Gaines in my life.

CHAPTER FIVE

"This is so bor-ing," Donna groused in this irritating singsong voice she used sometimes.

We were sitting in the hall outside the nurse's office three days later, waiting for our annual physical, which would certify we could be cheerleaders. It was some kind of stupid state law that all kids on athletic teams had to have the exam, which included us cheerleaders. At public school, they just expect you to come in with a form filled out that you had gotten permission to do sports. At Covington, they hired their own doctor to come in and tend to us pampered puppies.

"At least we're getting out of gym," Lindsey said philosophically, checking her French manicure. "Volleyball is so excruciating."

"Donna?" the nurse's assistant said, sticking her head out the door. "You can go in now."

"Finally!" Donna said, and she went inside.

I would be next. I pushed some hair behind one ear and felt the sweat at my temples. I knew I was running a low-grade fever, but I'd gotten used to it over the last few weeks. I'd gotten used to a lot of things—aching joints, exhaustion, weakness. So far I'd been able to keep it a secret—most of the time I didn't even let myself think about it. But what if I couldn't fool the doctor? Or even worse, what if something was really, seriously wrong with me?

I leaned my head back against the cool wall while Lindsey prattled on about some freshman guy at Vanderbilt who was hot to get in her pants. Finally, I was called into the clinic.

"Hi, Amber, how are you?" Candy Croller, the pretty, plump school nurse, greeted me.

"Just fine," I said, a big smile on my face.

"Great. This won't take long, honey, and you can get back to class. You want to hop up on the scale for me?"

I knew I'd lost weight, but I didn't know how much. I remembered that the year before at my physical, I'd taken my shoes off. This time I kept them on.

"One hundred seven," Candy read, then she

noted it on my chart. "Goodness! You've lost ten pounds since last year!"

Ten. And I'd kept my shoes on. That meant it had to be more like twelve, and I hadn't needed to lose an ounce. "I've been dieting," I lied.

"Well, I'm just pea-green jealous," Candy said with a sigh. "I'm getting so fat my thighs French kiss every time I take a step!" She wrapped the blood-pressure cuff around my arm and pumped, watching the numbers carefully. "You're just as healthy as can be!" she chirped. "Right as rain."

"Of course," I said with a smile, rolling down the sleeve of my denim shirt.

"Okey-dokey, Dr. Pinion will be here in just a minute for a look-see," Candy said, ushering me into the small rear room.

I didn't wait more than five minutes before Dr. Pinion came in carrying my chart. "Hello, there, young lady," he said, searching my chart for my name. "Uh . . . Amber, is it?"

"That's right," I said. In rapid succession he listened to my lungs and my heart, looked into my ears and down my throat, and tested my reflexes by thumping on my knees with a little rubber hammer. Then he felt the glands on the sides of my neck.

"Sore here?"

"Just a little," I lied. Actually, it hurt a lot.

"Been feeling tired lately?" he asked, his fingers still probing my neck.

I shrugged. "I'm really busy—I run around a lot."

He picked up a thermometer and stuck it under my tongue, then watched the digital read-out as it registered my temperature. "A little over a hundred," he said, throwing out the disposable thermometer covering.

"My mom had the flu last week," I lied. "I guess I got it from her."

"Has your throat been hurting?"

"Nope."

"Any other problems or pain?" he continued. "An achy feeling?"

"Nope," I lied again.

Dr. Pinion looked skeptical and went to the door. "Candy, would you do a blood test on Amber, please?"

"What do you need a blood test for?" I asked.

"Just covering the bases, young lady. Probably you're right and it's a touch of the flu, but I want to make sure you don't have mononucleosis."

"Mono?" I repeated, dumbfounded. "I can't

65

have mono. Don't you have to stay in bed with mono?"

"Let's not jump to any conclusions," the doctor said, patting my hand. "It's a simple test that can be run in my office this afternoon. I'll have the results for you by tomorrow. Meanwhile, I want you to take it easy."

"Take it easy like what?" I asked. "I've got cheerleading practice after school today for the away game with Montgomery Bell. I can't miss that."

"Sorry, young lady, but you are going to have to miss that," Dr. Pinion said, writing quickly in my records. "In fact, I'm sending you home until we get the results of the blood test. If you've got the flu, you need to be home in bed a couple of days, anyway. And if it's mononucleosis, it's highly contagious. But we'll cross that bridge if we come to it."

"I really don't feel sick—" I began.

"Do you have a way to get home?" he asked, ignoring my protests.

"My mother's car is in the shop," I fibbed. Actually, my mother's junk heap was in our back yard out by the creek, and it hadn't run for six years.

"Another relative? A friend?" the doctor asked. "Or else I'll tell someone from the principal's office to see that you get a taxi."

I could see there was no getting out of going home. "I suppose I could get my boyfriend to drive me, if you'll give him a pass," I said reluctantly. "He's in geometry, Room 211."

"Fine," Dr. Pinion agreed, scribbling something out and handing it to Candy. "And don't kiss your young man until we get the results of your test," he warned me.

Oh, well, this is just great, I thought dismally to myself as I sat near the front door of the school waiting for Richmond to bring his car around from the parking lot. The only good news I could think of was that I'd already finished the Sizzle video and mailed it off to *Star Search*. At least my career would be blossoming while I was home lying in bed like a slug.

"Do you need help, babycakes?" Richmond asked solicitously, jumping out of the car and hurrying over to me.

"Quit hovering," I snapped, pulling open the car door for myself. "It's the flu, is all."

"But the doctor said it might be mono," Richmond reminded me. As if I needed to be reminded.

67

"Well, it's not," I told him. "If I had mono, I'd know it. It's the flu."

"You'll be better for the game, won't you?" he asked, flicking a look at me when he stopped at a red light.

"Of course," I said. "This whole thing is just stupid."

Richmond talked about the football team's strategy for the upcoming game, and soon he was pulling up in front of my house. Immediately he got out of the car and came around to my side.

"What do you think you're doing?" I asked him, as I quickly got out of the car by myself.

"I'm attempting to be a gentleman and help my girlfriend who has the flu into the house, if that's all right with you," he replied, reaching for my elbow.

"It's not all right," I shot back, pulling my elbow away from him. "I'm not an invalid."

"But—"

"But nothing," I saw the hurt on his face, and I forced myself to smile at him sweetly. "I don't mean to be a grouchy ole thing, sweetheart," I cooed. "Ignore me—I get totally hateful when I'm sick."

"Aw, Amber . . ." Richmond reached for me, but I stepped away.

"Can't, Richie, not until the blood test comes back, but you know I'm dying for you." I blew him a kiss and made my way into the house.

"Momma?" I called, throwing my purse and my school books on the kitchen counter. As usual, Momma had left the house a mess. I put some dishes in the sink, then I put the tea kettle on the stove to boil. One of the many things I'd lied to the doctor about was my throat hurting. It did. I thought tea might help.

So, I was sitting there, feeling miserable, when I thought I heard a sound coming from my bedroom. Maybe Momma was napping and had just woken up when she heard me, is what I thought, so I got up to go see. Then another sound stopped me.

A moan. A sexy moan. A man's moan.

"Momma?" I called again, really loudly this time.

"Amber-Lynn?" I heard my mother gasp. Then some low talking I couldn't make out, then there was Momma, coming out of *my* bedroom, nervously tying the sash on her cotton flowered wrapper.

"Who the hell is in there?" I demanded.

"Baby? Why aren't you at school?" she asked anxiously.

"I got sent home with the flu," I told her. "I can see I wasn't expected."

"Now, Amber-Lynn—"

"Who the hell is in there?"

"Why, of course it's J.J., Amber-Lynn!" Momma said, her hand fluttering nervously at the neckline of her wrapper.

"What do you mean 'of course it's J.J.'?" I spat out. "You and J.J. were doing it in my bed? My bed?"

"We didn't think—" Momma began.

"I *know* you didn't think!" I screamed. "You two are so disgusting!"

"Don't be calling your momma names," J.J. said, zipping up his jeans as he walked out of my bedroom. He headed right to the refrigerator and took out a beer.

"I don't believe this!" I screeched.

"Do you have a fever, baby?" Momma asked, coming over to feel my forehead. The tea kettle began to whistle harshly, and Momma took it off the burner. "Why don't you get into bed, baby, and I'll bring you a nice cup of—"

"If I get into that bed that the two of you just got out of, I will vomit," I spat at her.

"You've got it all wrong, honey," Momma said, pulling the tea bags out of the cupboard to make me my cup of tea. "J.J. and me, we were celebrating somethin' real special. We're engaged-to-be-engaged!"

"You're kidding," I said dully.

"No, baby! It's true!" Momma said, her eyes shining brightly. She held her hand in my face, fingers extended proudly, so I could see the new ring she sported on her wedding ring finger—a narrow fake gold band with a red heart-shaped piece of glass stuck in the middle of it.

"Momma, you're thirty-two years old," I said, wiping the sweat from my temples with the back of my hand. "Thirty-two-year-old women don't get engaged-to-be-engaged."

"See, your trouble, girl, is you got no romance in you," J.J. opined, leaning against the counter and chugging back his beer.

"What, is that piece of glass supposed to keep her stringing along for another decade or so?" I asked him.

"I'll just go change the sheets on your bed,

baby," Momma said, scurrying into the bedroom, "and get you all settled in nice."

J.J. downed the last of his beer and reached into the refrigerator for another. He must have brought them with him—we didn't keep any alcohol in the house, usually.

"I thought you quit," I said, staring distastefully at him.

"You thought wrong," J.J. answered.

"If you get soused and hurt her again, J.J., I swear, I'll—"

"You'll what?" he challenged me belligerently.

I stared at him wordlessly, wishing I could crush him underneath my shoe like the cockroach he was.

"You don't seem to understand that I care for your momma and she cares for me," J.J. continued in a gentler tone. "If you was any kind of a daughter, you'd be happy for us."

"Come on and lay down, baby," Momma coaxed from the doorway. She leaned over to kiss me and I pulled away. "You shouldn't," I said. "The doctor said it might be mono, which is contagious."

"Mononucleosis?" Momma gasped, horrified. "Oh, my poor baby—"

"Please do not carry on," I said tiredly, moving past her into my bedroom. "It's not like I'm crippled for life or something." I shut the door and quickly undressed, pulling an oversized T-shirt over my head. Suddenly I was completely exhausted, so tired I could hardly stand. I crawled into bed, trying desperately not to think about what had been going on in that bed a few minutes ago.

I heard a knock on the door, and then Momma came in with my tea. She sat down next to me and stroked my forehead with her cool hand.

"Where's J.J.?" I asked, my eyes closed.

"He's gone, baby," Momma said. "I'm real sorry you walked in on that. I never would have . . ."

"I know," I sighed.

"I'm gonna call in sick and stay home with you tonight, look after you," Momma said, still stroking my forehead.

"You don't need to—"

"Yes, I do," Momma said firmly. "You just rest, baby. And call me if you need anything."

Momma tiptoed out of the room. I sat up a little, and took a sip of the tea. A pile in the corner caught my eye.

It was the sheets. Momma and J.J.'s dirty sheets.

I could still see that pile when I closed my eyes to sleep.

CHAPTER SIX

Richmond was coming at me, but he looked kind of like J.J., and he had this crazed kind of look in his eyes, and a huge, soiled sheet in his hands.

"You said you'd give me everything, now it's time to pay up!" his voice rumbled menacingly.

"No, no, I don't want to—"

"Yes, you do. You know you do. You're just like your mother!" He lifted the sheet and wrapped it around my head in a vise, so I couldn't breathe. I was choking, suffocating, gasping for breath, until my ears started ringing and ringing and . . .

Riiiiing!

I flew awake and sat up in bed, my heart pounding in my chest. The phone was ringing incessantly in the living room.

I grabbed it on the fifth ring. "Hello?"

"Hi, is this Amber Harkin?"

"Yes, yes, it is," I said, clearing the sleep out of my voice.

"This is Dr. Pinion's office. Hold just a moment for the doctor."

I glanced over at the kitty-cat clock with the rhinestone hands that Momma had won at bingo. It was noon. I'd been sleeping for fourteen hours.

"This is Dr. Pinion," he said when he came on the line. "I have the results of your blood test."

"Yes," I managed, grabbing the phone harder. *Please don't let me have mono,* I prayed. *I simply cannot have mono.*

"Your test for mononucleosis was negative," he told me.

"Oh, that's great!" I said, instantly feeling as if a huge weight had been lifted off of me.

"But the CBC also shows a rise in the rheumatoid factor in your blood," the doctor continued.

"What are you talking about?"

"It's probably nothing," Dr. Pinion continued smoothly. "But I'd like you to see a rheumatologist to have some more tests."

"What kind of tests?" I asked. "I've got the flu, right?"

"As I said, it probably is just the flu," Dr. Pinion assured me, "but there is this abnormally high R.A. factor in the latex test. Your titer is showing quite a high number. I'd like to see the test repeated, as well as a SED rate, a PCV, possibly a WBC . . ."

I felt dizzy, as if I'd just guzzled down two glasses of champagne or something. "Look, I have absolutely no idea what you're talking about, Dr. Pinion," I managed to choke out.

"Right, of course," Dr. Pinion agreed. "So sorry, young lady. I'm sure you're just fine, but I do want you to see this rheumatologist as soon as possible. Do you have a pen?"

"What's a rheumatologist?" I asked him as I hunted for a pen.

"A type of internal medicine specialist," he said, and then gave me the name and phone number of a Dr. James Major at St. Thomas Hospital. "How are you feeling?" Dr. Pinion added. "Any fever?"

"No, I feel much better," I said. Another lie. I felt dizzy and sweaty, and I ached all over. I was barely strong enough to hold myself up.

"Well, good," the doctor said cheerfully. "But you have your parents make an appointment with Dr. Major just to be on the safe side."

I assured him I would, and hung up the phone. Then I padded back into the bedroom, slipped the doctor's name and number into my journal, and got back in bed.

I heard the front door open, and then Momma was standing in the doorway. "Hey, sweetie-pie, you're awake!"

"Yeah," I said, sitting up against the pillows.

"Kayla drove me over to the Kroger, and I got you some chicken noodle soup," she told me. "Want me to heat you up some?"

"Sure," I said, and attempted a smile.

"Hey, my girl is smiling, you must be feeling better!" Momma exclaimed.

"Yeah, I really do," I told her.

"Well, you're probably just all run down, baby, you're always so go-go-go all the time," Momma admonished me.

She bustled into the kitchen, and when I heard her singing "I Fall to Pieces," her favorite song, I knew it was safe to peek a look at that doctor's name. No way was I going to see some specialist to have some stupid tests. For one thing, all that was wrong was that I had the flu. For another thing, we didn't have any medical insurance. No way could Momma afford for me to go see some specialist. I just had to be okay, that was all there was to it.

I stayed in bed and slept through the next day, and that Thursday I woke up feeling completely normal. Nothing hurt. I wasn't tired. No fever. I jumped out of bed and ran to call Richmond.

"Remington residence," the housekeeper answered the phone.

"May I speak to Richmond, please?" I asked in a hushed voice so I wouldn't wake Momma, who was sound asleep on the pull-out bed in the living room.

"Just one minute, please," she said, and went to get him.

"Hello?"

"Richie, sugar, it's me!"

"Hey, Amber! Why are you whispering?"

"I don't want to wake my mother," I told him. "Listen, I'm over the flu! I feel completely better!"

"That's great, babe!" Richmond exclaimed.

"Pick me up for school?"

"You betcha!" he agreed. "I'll be there the usual time. I've really missed you," he added.

"Me, too," I whispered, a big grin on my face. It just felt so good to feel normal again! I quickly jumped in the shower and then put on one of my favorite outfits—skinny white jeans, a sleeveless white T-shirt and a patterned silk man's vest over it. My jeans were falling a bit towards my hip bones, but that was the style, anyway. I blew my hair dry the best I could (it takes forever to dry), and ran out front just as Richmond's Miata was pulling up in front.

"Hey, Sleeping Beauty!" Richmond said, giving me a hug. "You look like a million!"

"Put the top down, sugar," I said, giving Richmond a brilliant smile. I slipped a cassette in and cranked up the volume. The still-warm fall air finished drying my hair, and I sang along with Mariah Carey all the way to school. I felt fabulous.

"You're back!" Donna cried when I walked into English class. She gave me a quick hug and then shook her head. "Honestly, you don't look like you were sick at all!"

"I'm healthy as a horse," I told her, smoothing my hair back over my shoulders. "What did I miss?"

"Not much," Donna said. "We just did the easy cheers at cheerleader practice because you weren't there to do the tough ones. Oh, and get this! Kyle broke up with Bitsy Renfrey—"

"That doesn't surprise me," I said, not showing how happy I felt at the news. I flipped through our English textbook to the poetry section, which is what we were studying.

"So guess who he's going out with now," Donna said significantly.

"Who?" I murmured nonchalantly, still looking through my book.

"Suzanne Lafayette, that's who!" Donna crowed.

I stared at her. "Miss Prim-and-Proper Suzanne Lafayette?"

Donna nodded eagerly. "Suzanne invited Kyle to a dance at the country club, and Kyle went. Bitsy was there and saw them, and I heard she ran off crying to the ladies' room and wouldn't come out the whole night."

"I could care less," I said coolly, and turned a page in my book. Okay, inside, I admit it, I was just boiling. So Kyle was going out with Richmond's old girlfriend. She was a stuck-up goody-goody type with the sex appeal of a dead carp. She looked like she was born wearing a string of real pearls and a dinky cashmere sweater, clutching her official blue-blood papers from the Daughters of the Confederacy in her red little fist. Her daddy was attorney general of the state of Tennessee and her momma was always mentioned in the society columns. Kyle would never accuse *her* of being a tramp. He'd never say she was just like her slutty mo—

"Amber!" Donna cried. "You're ripping the page out of your book!"

I looked down, and sure enough I tensed my hand up so much that the page it was holding was all crumpled and ragged. Before I could make up some excuse the bell rang, and Ms. Levine started talking about the imagery in Elizabeth Barrett Browning's poetry.

I vowed to put Kyle Gaines completely out of my mind, and I did. At lunchtime I called Crater and told him I was all better, and I'd be in to teach my advanced aerobics class right after school. Naturally he sounded thrilled to death to hear from me. I arranged with Donna and Cassie to have a Sizzle rehearsal right after that. My life was back on schedule. Everything was fine, perfect, terrific. I felt so good that it was easy to forget about what Dr. Pinion had said. After all, what with so many people suing doctors these days, I figured he was just trying to cover his butt. Certainly if I felt so absolutely normal, nothing could really be wrong with me.

"Amber-Lynn, come here and give me some sugar!" Crater cried when I walked into the dance studio after school. He put his mammoth arms around me in a huge bear hug and swung me around the room. I could hardly believe it—I knew Crater was glad I was back, but usually he was real shy around me. This was a whole new attitude. "I got some news on the phone not five minutes ago, girl, that you are not going to believe."

"What?" The only thing I could imagine getting that excited about was *Star Search,* and I knew he wouldn't know whether we'd been picked because my phone number was the contact number I'd sent in.

"You ever hear tell of Tanya Tucker? Vince Gill? Or maybe Alan Jackson?" he asked, naming some of the biggest country music stars in the world.

"No, Crater, I've been living under a rock," I replied.

"How'd you like to perform with them?" he asked gleefully.

"What are you talking about?" I asked, pulling my sweatshirt over my head.

"I'm fixing to tell you that, Amber-Lynn. But you got to sit down so I can have your undivided attention."

I sat. "Crater, I have to teach a class in five minutes," I reminded him impatiently.

"How about Garth Brooks? You ever hear tell of him?" Crater crowed.

"You're making me nuts, Crater. Cut to the chase."

"Well, here's the deal," Crater said slowly. "This fellow I'm weight training is head of the Arthritis Foundation, and their telethon is coming up next week. I told him about Sizzle, and I done gave him a copy of your *Star Search* audition tape—I hope that was okay?"

I nodded. "Go on."

"Well, he loved it! He wants ya'll to be on TV!" Crater exclaimed. "And all them stars, they're all appearing in the telethon, too!"

"Is it national?" I asked quickly.

"Danged if it ain't!" Crater whooped. "Last year they done it from Los Angeles, but this year they got all these big country stars involved, so the whole thing is being done right at the Opry!"

"Sizzle is going to be on national TV?" I asked faintly.

"Next Monday night," Crater said. "He wanted to know could ya'll go on around eleven and do two numbers. I know it's short notice, and I know it's kind of a late time slot, but—"

"Crater, you are such a sweetheart!" I yelled, throwing my arms around him.

"Aw, well . . ." Crater blushed so hard the pits in his complexion stood out like a relief map.

"You are a wonderful friend," I said, kissing him on the cheek.

The time dragged through my aerobics class until finally Donna and Cassie showed up for rehearsal. They both went crazy when I told them the news.

"This is totally awesome!" Donna screamed. "Wait until everyone hears about this!"

"We're going to have to really rehearse between now and then," Cassie warned. "I'm sure we're rusty because of the time you took off."

"I had the flu," I said in measured tones. "I didn't just take time off."

"Well, whatever," Cassie shrugged. "The results are the same."

"Let's get to work, then," I suggested, swallowing all the nasty things I wanted to yell at Cassie. Just who the hell did she think she was, anyway? The witch was still on probation, as far as I was concerned!

We worked on "Buff Enough" first, which I figured would be one of our TV numbers. It didn't take me long to realize I didn't really have all of my energy back, but I'd be damned if I'd let on to Cassie Stewart. I forced myself to work that much harder, pushing myself even when I felt like just falling over.

And I could feel her watching me, studying me, and I knew she knew.

"Wow, that was great!" Donna exclaimed after our fourth time through. "We are the hottest!" She reached for her towel and wiped the perspiration off her neck.

"I thought it lacked energy," Cassie said. She stared at me. "Are you still getting over your flu?"

"Thanks for your concern," I said, my voice dripping sarcasm, "but I'm fine."

"I just noticed that at the last few rehearsals before you got sick, you were looking kind of lackluster," she pointed out.

"Well, I guess I was already coming down with the flu then and I didn't know it," I replied.

"Oh, come on, ya'll, we were great that time!" Donna protested.

"We were okay," Cassie said, giving me an appraising look. "Amber's extension is soft on the one-armed push-ups."

She was right. When we went into the one-armed, power push-ups I felt that old weakness in my wrist, and I couldn't completely straighten out my arm without it trembling so much that it felt as if it would give way.

"Why don't you just worry about the syncopated section where you snap your head back a beat late," I suggested, getting up from the floor. "Let's do it again."

We worked on and on, until I felt like throwing up or fainting, but I never let it show. It was like a contest between Cassie and me—I knew that now. Whoever showed weakness would lose. Donna had been right about her all along. Well, I was tougher than Cassie Stewart, no matter how tired I felt. I could handle her.

"I feel like I'm dying," Donna moaned, after we'd been working for four hours without a break. She fell on her back on the floor and put her towel over her head.

"We need another half hour," I insisted.

"We've got to get the ending right on 'Beat Street.' "

"I'm sorry, but I feel like road kill," Donna groaned. "And I've still got two hours of geometry to do when I get home. Can't we work tomorrow?"

"I suppose," I sighed, my back to Cassie and Donna. My legs were trembling so hard with exhaustion that I could barely stand, but I refused to let them see. I had an out—I'd just blame it on Donna. "We'll meet here tomorrow, same time," I commanded, turning around to face them.

"If you're up to it," Cassie said, stepping into her sweat pants.

"It's not me I'm worried about," I snapped back at her.

"Yeah, right," Cassie said softly. She put her gym bag over her shoulder and walked out of the studio.

"I'm outta here," Donna said, waving goodbye and hurrying after Cassie.

I sat down on the bench and stared at the floor. Practically overnight Cassie had gone from being afraid to stand up to me because I could kick her out of the group, to challenging everything. It had to be because she knew how good she was, how much better Sizzle was with her in it. She knew I cared too much about succeeding to kick her out of the group. I didn't have anyone nearly as good to replace her with. But somehow, like a predatory animal, she was sensing a weakness in me. I knew I had to stand up to her, no matter what.

No matter what.

CHAPTER SEVEN

Crater gave me a ride home, and I knew in the car that I was running a fever again. The sweat had turned to chills, and I hurt everywhere. I ignored it. Crater and I talked about Sizzle's opportunity to be on TV, which of our outfits we should wear, things like that. Usually I wore his admiration like a fur coat, but right at that moment my mind was not having the same conversation as my mouth.

As I chatted on confidently about Sizzle, all I was really thinking about was crawling into bed with every blanket in the house on me.

Fortunately Momma had already left for work so I didn't have to try to hide how sick I felt. I dragged myself into the bedroom and crawled under the blankets with my sweats on, all curled up in a ball. That's how I fell asleep, and I didn't wake up until the next morning.

Everything hurt. I felt as if I'd been run over by a truck. I went to put my hands down on the bed, to brace myself into a sitting position, only I couldn't.

My right hand, you see, didn't work.

I looked down at it. My wrist was red and puffy-looking. My fingers seemed swollen. It looked and felt like someone else's hand.

I told my fingers to flex. Nothing happened.

A feeling of panic swept over me. This was just too weird! It couldn't be happening! I concentrated all my energy on my right hand, and slowly my fingers began to close about a half an inch. And that was all.

I told my wrist to flex. Nothing happened.

I'm just stiff from working so hard, is what I told myself. *I'll feel better once I take a shower.*

I swung my legs over the side of the bed, which made my head throb horribly. With my left hand, I braced myself enough to stand. Pain shot through my legs, my ankles, my feet. Moaning and crying, I hobbled my way into the shower.

The blessed shower. As the hot water cascaded over my painful joints, I could feel the pain easing and some mobility returning. I tried flexing my right hand, and found I could. My wrist was better, too. After ten minutes the hot water ran out, but I was feeling much better. So I really had just overdone my workout my first day up after the flu. That's all it was. That's all I'd let it be.

I moved slowly getting dressed, but at least I could move. I popped three aspirin and soon felt myself sweating out my low-grade fever. I felt tired and weak, but I was ready when Richmond pulled up to drive me to school.

On the outside, I looked completely normal. As the day progressed, no one knew that I felt like falling over with exhaustion, that just holding a pen to write made my fingers scream with pain, that when I walked it felt as if someone were driving burning needles into my heels. No one knew. And I wasn't going to let anyone know.

Aerobics class. How was I going to teach aerobics class? It's amazing what the body can do when it's forced to do it. I simply refused to give in. I drank three cups of black coffee, popped four aspirin, and taught the class.

By the time Donna and Cassie showed up for Sizzle rehearsal, my bravado began to fail me. I had never felt the kind of pain that was coursing through my body.

"You're looking kind of feverish," Cassie said as she stretched out at the barre.

"I'm fine," I lied, gripping the tabletop under the cassette player tightly. "I just taught an aerobics class." I took a step and almost stumbled.

"You okay, Amber?" Donna asked, coming over to me.

"Sure," I said. "I just need to throw some cold water on my face." I walked to the ladies' room, and because I could feel their eyes on me I refused to limp, I just refused. Then I locked myself in a stall and cried.

Because something was really, really wrong.

I was not going to be able to get through a Sizzle rehearsal. I was going to have to tell them.

I washed my face, took a deep breath, and headed back out to the studio. "Listen, ya'll, I must have gotten up too soon from this flu thing," I said, as if it were a minor annoyance.

"We need to rehearse," Cassie stated flatly.

"Well, she can't rehearse if she's sick, can she?" Donna shot at Cassie. She turned to me. "It's okay, we'll work tomorrow," she assured me.

"If you think you'll be better tomorrow," Cassie said. "We've only got Saturday and Sunday to rehearse before the telethon—"

"I know that," I said. "I'm sure I just need a little rest. I'll absolutely be here tomorrow. Crater told me we can have the small studio at twelve, he'll move the beginners aerobics in here."

"You want me to drive you home?" Donna asked solicitously.

"We're staying to rehearse," Cassie informed Donna. I was too tired to fight her.

"I'll ask Crater for a ride, no problem," I said quickly.

"Oh, okay," Donna said, turning back to the mirror. How easily she was following Cassie's directions. As easy as she usually followed mine.

"See you tomorrow," Cassie called, going through the cassettes. "If you're better, that is."

Crater got his assistant, Greg, to watch the front desk, and he drove me home, as kind as can be. This time I was too exhausted and sick to even pretend to make small talk with him. I just laid my head back on the seat and closed my eyes.

When we pulled up to my house, I noticed Kayla's car parked in front. That meant Momma and Kayla must have just come back from some-where or other. I desperately didn't want to see anyone.

"Bye, Crater," I managed to say as I got out of his car. "Thanks for the ride."

"You take care, you hear?" Crater told me before he drove off.

"Hi, Momma," I whispered as I dragged myself in the front door. She and Kayla were sitting at the kitchen table with a Ouija board between them.

"Hey, sweet pea!" Momma said, not looking up from the board. "Me and Kayla were just down to the Kroger, and the cutest little girls from Church of Christ had a table set up right in front, selling old toys and books and things to raise money for new choir robes, and they had this here Ouija board on sale for only one dollar!"

"The only thing it's missing is the little triangle doohickey that's supposed to travel across the board," Kayla said, also not looking up from the game. "So we're using a quarter."

I looked down, and sure enough each of them had two fingers on a quarter that sat in the middle of the board.

"It hasn't moved," Momma informed me. "Maybe we ain't concentrating our energy enough."

"'Or maybe it's because we bought it from Church of Christ," Kayla mused. "A Ouija board might be against their religion."

"Well, it's not against *my* religion," Momma said. "I want this quarter to tell me when J.J. is gonna actually propose."

"When pigs fly," I mumbled and walked slowly into my room, falling over on the bed. I closed my eyes and wished I was somewhere, anywhere, besides this crappy old shack with Momma playing with her dollar Ouija board in the living room.

"Amber-Lynn?" Momma asked, coming to the door. "Are you feeling poorly?"

"Nice of you to notice," I said flatly.

"I'm sorry, baby," Momma said, instantly contrite. She sat down next to me and stroked my forehead. "Is it your flu come back?" she asked me.

I nodded pitifully.

"Maybe we should go down to the clinic," Momma said, referring to the free clinic nearby, where poor people went for medical care.

I'd been there twice, once for the measles, once for strep throat. The time I went with strep throat I was so sick. The nurse treated me like just because I was poor, I was also stupid, and spoke to me as if I was mentally deficient. And this rich doctor, who volunteered to work there one day a week out of the goodness of his heart, he acted like I should be so grateful that he'd spend time on someone like me. The strep throat hurt like hell, but not as much as they made me hurt. I vowed I'd never go there again.

"It's just the flu," I whispered. "I just need to rest."

"You're sure those mono tests were negative?" Momma asked, her voice filled with worry.

"I'm sure."

She looked at her Timex. "I've got to get ready for work, baby. I can't miss any more time."

"It's okay," I told her. "I'm going to be asleep, anyway."

"You want Kayla to stay with you? Or how about if she asks Kyle to come on over for a spell?"

"God, no," I groaned. "I'm fine."

"Well, if you're sure." She stroked my forehead silently for a minute or two. "Do you think the Ouija will work with a quarter?" she finally asked me.

"Sure," I told her. She gave me a huge smile of relief, kissed my cheek and tiptoed out of my room.

I was asleep before she got to the door.

CHAPTER EIGHT

I've never been sure if I believe in God. It wasn't a subject I ever gave a lot of thought to, until that weekend before Sizzle was supposed to be on the telethon, and then I was praying for all I was worth that I'd be all better in time to be on TV.

Even though I'd told Cassie I'd be at rehearsal the next day, no way could I get out of bed. Not the following day, either, and the night after that was the night of the telethon.

And then, like a miracle, I woke up Monday morning feeling fine, totally ready to rock 'n' roll. Now I look back on those prayers and see how ridiculous they were. But I see a lot of things differently, now.

Anyway, Monday I went to school and met with Cassie and Donna right afterwards to work on the two numbers we'd be doing on TV that night. I was a little rusty and a little weak, but I was as determined as a body can be, ready for my first taste of stardom. By the time we were done rehearsing, we all felt as positive as could be. We were *good*.

Richmond borrowed his parents' Rolls-Royce, and he drove Cassie, Donna, and me to the Grand Ole Opry, where the telethon was being held. Bobby Pratt came along, too. He and Donna spent the entire trip in the backseat sucking face. Cassie's boyfriend didn't come, on account of he was a sophomore at Yale, which is on the other side of the world, in Connecticut. Richmond kept rubbing my thigh and telling me how excited he was and how I was going to be a bigger star than Madonna and Paula Abdul. The way he figured it Madonna was over the hill and Paula had thunder thighs for days, whereas I was perfect. Since I was the one who had convinced him I was perfect in the first place, I just smiled enigmatically, which may have passed for humility.

At the first checkpoint that leads into the private parking lot for staff and talent, we gave our names to the guard. For just a moment as he looked down that list I held my breath, certain that our names wouldn't be there, that we'd be turned away. But no, the man checked us off and waved us through.

The five of us walked in the stage door, and stood there waiting to give our names to the inside guard. As we were standing there, Garth Brooks walked right by us. The guard waved, and Garth waved, and he walked right by, nodding his head at me in a friendly fashion.

"Oh my God, oh my God, I'm going to die," Donna said, grabbing my arm so tight I knew I'd bruise up from her fingerprints. "That was Garth Brooks. Garth Brooks just flirted with you."

"He didn't flirt with me, he nodded to me, one professional to another," I explained patiently.

"You mean he already knows who you are?" Donna asked, wide-eyed.

Sometimes that girl pained me.

"No, Donna. But if I am backstage with two tons of makeup on my face, carrying a costume over my arm, it's a good bet that I'm a performer."

We gave our names and were assigned to a dressing room down the hall, which we found easily. The room next door to us was open, and I saw Tanya Tucker in there playing with her baby,

Presley. She waved the baby's hand at us and smiled as we walked by. Even Cassie was impressed, though I could see she was doing her best to act nonchalant.

"You two go gawk at something else, we need to change in here," Cassie told the guys, shooing them out into the hall. They were only too happy to go and star-gaze.

We'd agreed to wear our sexiest, showiest outfit, which Donna's parents had paid to have made the year before. It consisted of a silver lace bodysuit with silver lightning bolts made of sequins and rhinestones that appeared random but were actually strategically designed to cover what has to be covered. We made up our eyes with false eyelashes and black eyeliner, and wore pale, almost silver lipstick. Donna had argued that maybe our outfits should be baggy, since that was the current style. But I argued that that was the perfect reason to do the opposite—that people were getting tired of seeing girls dancing around in clothes that were three sizes too big. I figured this is the kind of logic Madonna used to make herself into a star. Always try to keep one step ahead of the pack. You can't ever be scared to be different.

We moved the chairs over to one side of the room and did our warm-ups against the wall. I couldn't help noticing how hot Cassie looked in the silver outfit. Her red hair waved perfectly over one eye as she leaned over into a waist stretch. She seemed completely cool and collected.

A stage manager knocked on our door and told us we'd be on in a half-hour, and if we wanted we could wait in the Green Room with the other talent.

"The other talent," Donna hissed to me after the stage manager left. "That means Garth. I want to get his autograph."

"Donna Martin," I said in a steely voice, "you are not going to ask Garth Brooks for his autograph in the Green Room at the Opry. It's totally tacky."

"I'm staying in here to warm up," Cassie told us, dropping into a split and bending her head down to her knee in one graceful, fluid motion.

Donna and I walked down the hall and found the Green Room, a large comfortable room with couches, coffee, and a deli buffet set up in the corner. Overhead there was a large TV, which showed the telethon. At the moment Bill Monroe, the father of bluegrass music, was out there playing the mandolin.

"I got Tanya Tucker's autograph!" Bobby Pratt said, rushing over to show us her scrawl on a napkin.

"How do we look?" Donna asked, twirling in a circle.

"Hotter than a pistol," Bobby told Donna, and then made a stupid growling sound, which made Donna giggle with excitement.

"Where's Richmond?" I asked Bobby.

"He's in the hall talking to one of the backup singers," Bobby said, his hands circling Donna's waist. "Don't worry, though, she's not even in your league."

"Bobby, believe me, I wasn't worried," I said dryly.

Then, right there in the Green Room in front of Vince Gill, Mary-Chapin Carpenter, and a bunch of musicians, Bobby stuck his tongue down Donna's throat. Now, I myself have been accused of ostentatious behavior, but never tastelessness. This little display was so tasteless I had to move to the other side of the room so as not to be associated with them.

I poured myself a glass of fruit juice from the

buffet and sat down next to a pretty little girl of about nine with a pink ribbon in her hair.

"Hi," she chirped, giving me a great smile.

"Hi," I answered, sipping the juice. "Is your momma or daddy in the show tonight?"

"No, I am," she said, excitement in her voice. "I love your costume! Are you a singer?"

"A dancer," I told her.

"You're really beautiful," she told me fervently.

I smiled. "Well, thanks, so are you," I told her, quite honestly. I wondered what talent a little kid like her could have that would put her on a telethon with all these big stars. "So, what's your talent?"

She thought about that a minute. "I'm pretty good at science," she finally said.

I laughed. "No, I mean what's your talent that you're doing in the telethon?"

She shrugged. "Oh, all I do is walk out there and talk to the lady with the microphone. It's not hard. I did it twice before."

That one stumped me. "But what do you talk about?" I asked her. "Does your gramma or grampa have arthritis or something?"

"Nope," the little girl said matter-of-factly. "I do."

"But you're a kid," I pointed out. "Only old people get arthritis."

"A lot of kids get it, too," she explained. "It's called juvenile rheumatoid arthritis. I'm the poster girl!"

She pointed to the wall, and there was a huge poster of her in a frilly white dress, advertising the arthritis telethon. I looked back over at her. She looked perfectly normal—no leg braces, no wheel chair.

"Does it hurt?" I asked her.

"Sometimes," she said with a shrug. "Hey, what's your name?"

"Amber. What's yours?"

"Caroline," she said, scrunching up her nose. "I hate it. I wish it was Jennifer."

"Caroline! There you are!" a harried-looking woman called, rushing over to us. "You're on in five minutes! We need to go backstage now!"

"That's my mother," Caroline told Amber. "She gets real nervous when I'm gonna be on TV."

"Come on, baby. I hope you didn't muss your dress!" her mother said anxiously.

"Mom, this is Amber," Caroline said, introducing me. "Isn't she beautiful?"

"Yes, baby, now let's get going," her mother said, not looking at me. "You know better than to sit for so long!" She leaned over to reach for Caroline, who blushed a deep red.

"Mom, I want to do it myself."

"But Caroline—"

Caroline shook her mother off, then slowly she leaned forward in the chair until she sort of rocked herself into a standing position. Then slowly, painfully, she began shuffling her legs across the room, inch by inch. Her mother hovered over her, but Caroline wouldn't let her mother touch her. She turned around to give me a smile. "Nice meeting you," she said.

"You, too," I called, and I watched as she worked her way across the room. She moved as if she were a ninety-year-old woman.

"Dang if you don't look good enough to eat," Richmond said, coming up from the opposite direction.

"Look at that kid," I whispered, watching Caroline leave. "Did you know kids can get arthritis?"

Richmond looked over at Caroline. "Nope. Poor kid." He turned back to me and traced a lazy finger from my mouth down to my lacy, silver cleavage. "I can't wait to get you alone after this thing," he whispered.

"Mmmmmm," I murmured promisingly, but really my mind was on Caroline until she disappeared around the corner.

"Sizzle, you're on in ten," the stage manager said, checking us off a list. "I need you backstage now."

"Can I come?" Richmond asked eagerly.

"Sure, *if* you stay back out of the way," the woman said curtly. "Follow me."

We found Donna and Cassie and followed the stage manager through the labyrinth of halls until we went through a heavy door with a flashing red light above it that read ON THE AIR.

And then, there we were, backstage at the Opry.

Now, I am not a big country music fan (although I did once have a dream that I got hot and heavy with Travis Tritt, and let me tell you, it is a dream I would not mind repeating), but it was impossible to actually be backstage at the Opry and not feel a special thrill. Garth Brooks was standing over in the corner wearing a baseball cap and a sweatshirt talking with Vince Gill, who was tuning his guitar. Tanya Tucker was standing on the other side of the stage, where her baby was playing patty-cakes with Mary-Chapin Carpenter. I thought about Momma, who lived and breathed country, and wished there was some way I could have brought her without having to introduce her to my friends. Well, there wasn't, so I'd have to remember every single detail to tell her when she got off work.

Talk-show host Ralph Emery and Marie Osmond were out onstage, talking to the audience. Caroline had just finished her segment, and Marie was making a pitch to send in money. Caroline caught my eye from the opposite wing, and waved at me with excitement. Her wave was stiff, as if her arm didn't bend right. I waved back.

"Okay, Sizzle," the stage manager said quietly, "Ralph Emery will introduce ya'll right after this pledge pitch. Your music will start, and you'll go right into your first number, then your second. After that, Ralph will come over to talk with you."

"We have to *talk?*" Donna hissed hysterically.

"I'll do the talking," I told her. Cassie gave me a cool look, but didn't say anything. I didn't really care what she thought—it was my group, not hers.

"Now we've got something really different for you, folks," Ralph was saying. "I haven't seen these little ladies myself, but they've been performing around Nashville, and I understand they're really wonderful dancers. Let's have a Grand Ole Opry welcome for Sizzle!"

The stage manager urged the audience to applaud from out of camera range, while the three of us ran onstage and took our places. My heart was pounding in my chest so loud I thought it would be heard over the music. And then the opening strains of "Buff Enough" filled the air, and I was gone.

Leaping, twirling, dancing for all I was worth. My arms stretched wider, and my legs kicked higher. I was on fire, adrenaline pumping through me. This was it, the highest high, the beginning of my new life, the end of my old one. Now the world would sit up and take notice, and that poor little girl would be buried forever and ever, amen. Everything was possible.

On the final sixteen bars we did the roll-over into the one-handed push-ups, our legs crossed over each other. There I was, front and center, doing them perfectly. All the way down without letting my weight fall, then a perfect extension, a sassy, sexy look on my face. Repeat the combination, and then the big finish, wham!

The applause, whistles, and cheers washed over me like solid love. This was it! This was everything! The bright lights bounced off our costumes as we bowed in unison. We took our places for our second number, "Man Handler," and moved into the opening formation after four beats of the drums. It was like magic, everything went absolutely perfectly. Donna took her solo, a double cartwheel into a round off. Then Cassie, aerial splits into a fly-over and a triple pirouette.

Now it was my solo.

I remember it as if it was a movie in my head that I could play over and over, every detail crystal clear. First I did a line of whirling turns across the stage, an arabesque leap, then a double backwards flip, a single forward, and a triple pirouette back to the center of the floor. I heard the audience gasp, and then applaud wildly.

We moved into the final syncopated section, the double-time ball-change where we each jumped into aerial splits, then slid across the floor in our final pose.

Now the applause was even stronger, people were stomping and cheering, and the three of us were breathing hard and bowing with huge grins on our faces. Ralph Emery came over to me and tried to talk, but the applause just got louder, and so he stepped back and gestured to us to take another bow.

I'll always remember that moment, when I stepped forward into the lights and bowed before all those cheering people at the Opry, and I knew all those other people were watching me on TV, all across the country. I'll always remember every single moment of that performance, down to the tiniest detail.

Because, you see, I know now what I didn't know then.

It would be the last time in my life I would ever be able to dance.

CHAPTER NINE

I woke up the next morning, and I couldn't move.

The best way I describe it is to say that it felt as if every bone in my body was broken. And I was scared. Before I'd at least been able to hobble into the shower, and then the warm water helped loosen me up, but this time there was no possibility of my going anywhere.

I had to pee. I knew I couldn't get to the bathroom. *Please, God, don't let this be happening to me,* I prayed. My prayers were not answered. It was happening.

"Momma?" I called. My voice sounded weak and pitiful. It was as if I didn't even have the energy it took to yell. I took a deep breath. "Momma?" I called again. But when Momma is sound asleep, it takes the devil to wake her. I knew she couldn't hear me. "Mommaaaaaaa!" I screamed as loud as I could.

I heard noises from the living room, and then Momma was standing in my doorway, squinting and pushing her hair out of her face. "Baby? What?"

"I'm sick," I whispered, and tears began to course down my cheeks. "I'm really, really sick, Momma."

"Oh, baby, what is it?" she asked, immediately running over to me and putting her hand on my forehead.

"It's not the flu, Momma, it's . . . I don't know what it is!" I cried.

"You didn't lie to me about your mono test, did you?" she asked anxiously.

"No, but . . ." I bit my lower lip, not wanting to continue.

"But what? You're scaring the daylights out of me, Amber-Lynn!"

Haltingly, I said, "The doctor, at school . . . told me something was wrong, with my blood—"

"Your blood?" Momma interrupted. Her hand flew over her mouth. "Oh, dear Jesus, that's leukemia!"

"No, no, he never said that!" I protested. "Hand me my journal from my drawer," I told her. She got it out and I clumsily tried to find the piece of paper I'd stuck in there where I'd written the information Dr. Pinion had given me. Finally, it fell out on its own when I dropped the book. "He told me I needed to see a rheumatologist. Look at that paper."

"What's a rheumatologist?" Momma asked.

"Some kind of internal medicine specialist is all he told me," I explained. "And he didn't say for sure anything was wrong with me, just that I needed more tests."

"But Amber-Lynn," Momma asked, "why on God's green earth didn't you tell me about this?"

"Because I was so sure nothing was wrong!" I cried. "I felt better, I went back to school . . ."

"Well, I'm calling this doctor right this minute," Momma said, and got up to do just that.

"Wait! I . . . I need to get to the bathroom," I muttered, gulping hard.

All the color drained out of Momma's face. "You can't . . .?"

"I can't do it alone," I admitted, choking back my tears.

Something shifted in Momma, and a steely resolve came to her face. "It's okay, baby," she said. "Can you get there if you lean on me?"

"I'll try," I said. Carefully, ever so slowly, I moved into a sitting position. Then Momma put her arms around me, I crossed my hands behind her neck, and she lifted my weight onto her. I'm three inches taller than Momma, but she didn't falter.

"That's fine, baby, you lean on me," she said. She half-carried me to the bathroom. Our progress was slow, as each faltering step brought excruciating pain to my feet, my legs, every joint in my body.

"Momma?" I whispered. "I can't do this . . ." There was no way I could lower my body to the toilet seat. I would have to bend my knees, and I couldn't do that.

"Just put your arms around my neck, and I'll lower you down," Momma said. Slowly, she maneuvered me down to the toilet seat, where I sat sobbing. "Oh, baby . . ." she said.

"Leave me alone!" I screamed. I knew I shouldn't be screaming at Momma, the only person who would help me, but I couldn't help myself. "Can I have a little privacy, please?"

"I'll be right outside the door," she told me, and left me there.

After I was done I was determined to stand up by myself and wash my face and brush my teeth. I refused to care about how much it hurt. So I told my body to stand up. But I couldn't. I simply didn't have the strength to move from a sitting position to a standing one. Maybe if the toilet had had some kind of handles, or if it wasn't so low to the ground. I simply could not get off the commode.

So I called Momma again, and she helped me get up and get back to bed, then she brought me a basin of water to wash with, and my toothbrush and toothpaste. The toothbrush felt as if it weighed ten pounds, it hurt my jaw to open my mouth far enough to brush my teeth. Pain shot through my elbows when I brought the wet washcloth to my face.

Meanwhile, Momma had taken the piece of paper with the doctor's name and number on it into the living room, and she was dialing his number. As much pain as I was in, I was also thinking about the terrible humiliation when Momma told this fancy doctor that we didn't have any insurance. The nurse would probably get that real fake sweet voice and say how regretful she was but the doctor didn't accept patients without insurance. Nothing personal.

"... It's about my daughter," I heard Momma saying into the phone. She explained that Dr. Pinion had told her to call to have more tests, then she was quiet, obviously listening. "No, three weeks from now will not be all right," Momma said firmly. "My child is in terrible pain, she cannot walk, and the doctor must see her today, this morning, right now! ... Yes. ... Yes. ... Thank you," Momma said, and hung up.

She came back into my room. "I'm gonna help you get dressed, baby. Then I'll throw on some clothes, and we're going straight over to St. Thomas Hospital to see this Dr. Major."

"How are we supposed to get to St. Thomas? Fly?"

"We'll get us a taxi," Momma said, scurrying back into the living room for her purse. "I've got four dollars here," she said, counting the money in her purse. "What have you got?"

"About two," I told her. "I didn't get my paycheck from Crater yet. Where are all your tips from Saturday night?" Like most waitresses, Momma made the vast majority of her money from tips. I knew she usually took in around seventy-five dollars on a Saturday night.

"You know me and Kayla always play bingo on Sunday," Momma said, opening my drawer to take out a pair of leggings for me.

"You spent it all on bingo cards?"

"Well, no," Momma said slowly, reaching down so I could step into the leggings. "J.J. needed a small loan to tide him over—"

"You gave that drunken bastard your tip money?" I yelled.

"Amber-Lynn, we are engaged-to-be-engaged now, and—"

"I don't want to hear it," I whispered, all the fight gone out of me.

"Don't you worry, baby," Momma said, helping me into a T-shirt. "I'm gonna get dressed and run over to Kayla's and ask can we borrow her car."

Five minutes later she came in wearing her skin-tight blue jeans and a too-tight T-shirt that read 100% CHOICE GRADE A FEMALE across her bosom. She kissed me on the forehead and ran out the door.

I lay back on the pillows, too tired and scared to even cry. What could be happening to me?

What if I was dying? I was so exhausted, I fell into a half-sleep, and then I was startled by a knock on the front door.

"Amber?" a deep voice called.

My eyes flew open. It was Richmond, picking me up for school. I had forgotten all about him.

"Don't come in!" I screamed frantically. "I'm . . . I'm contagious!" It was the first lie that popped into my head.

"Amber, you home?" Richmond yelled.

I knew he couldn't hear me, and I knew that Momma had left the door open when she'd run over to Kayla's, and I knew that all that stood between Richmond and me was a screen door with holes in it.

I also knew he would come in. He was going to see inside, and I was helpless to stop him.

I heard the door squeak, and his footsteps, and in my mind I saw what he must be seeing: the cracked, yellow linoleum, the cardboard taped over a hole in the wall, the plastic wrap on the back window, where the pane had broken, the peeling movie magazine pictures glued to the walls, the shabbiness and poverty and ugliness that I'd hidden from him, from everyone who mattered.

At that moment I didn't worry anymore that I was dying. I prayed to die.

And then he was standing at the foot of my bed, staring at me, shock and pity all mixed up on his face. "Amber?" he whispered.

"Get out," I muttered.

"I knocked and no one answered," he said, looking around my room as if he smelled something bad. "You actually live like this?"

"Get the hell out!" I screamed. "Get out!"

He stood there a moment, clearly not sure what he should do, and then I heard the door open, voices in the living room, and then there was Momma in her too-tight T-shirt and Kyle standing in the doorway, everybody staring at everybody, and I wanted to die all over again.

"You must be Amber's young man," Momma said, finding her voice. "I'm Sugaleen Harkin, Amber's momma, but you can call me Sugar. Everyone does."

I couldn't believe she said that to him. It was my worst nightmare come true.

"Nice to meet you," Richmond said automatically.

"And I guess you know Kyle here from school," Momma added.

"Right," Richmond said.

"Well, it's lovely to meet you, but I'm sorry it has to be because my daughter is feeling poorly," Momma said, tugging at the bottom of her T-shirt. It still left a half inch of fleshy white skin exposed above her jeans.

"I . . . I guess you're sick, so . . . I'll just be going," Richmond stammered, backing towards the door.

"Get Amber's homework for her," Kyle told him tersely.

"Sure, sure," Richmond agreed, now halfway out of my room. Momma and Kyle moved over to let him by. "Uh, it was nice to have met you," he added to Momma automatically, and then he hightailed for the front door.

"Well, I'm so embarrassed he met me without my face on!" Momma exclaimed, her hand fluttering to her cheek. "But he seemed to be a very polite young man."

"He's a horse's ass," Kyle snapped.

"Why, Kyle—" Momma protested.

"What the hell is *he* doing here?" I asked, pointing to Kyle.

"Kyle's going to drive us over to the hospital," Momma said. "Ain't that nice of him?"

"Can't we just borrow the car?"

"I thought some help would be good. . . ." Momma hesitated. "One person to park and one person to help you get in to the doctor's. . . ."

"I don't need any help!" I yelled.

"But, baby, you can't walk—" Momma began.

"Yes, I can," I said, and threw my legs over the side of the bed. As Kyle and Momma stared at me, I raised myself to my feet, and then using all my willpower I moved myself in a slow, agonizing shuffle towards the door.

CHAPTER TEN

By the time I was sitting in Dr. Major's waiting room at St. Thomas Hospital, I was white with fatigue. In some ways it seemed as if I felt less stiff when I moved around some, but on the other hand the smallest physical effort exhausted me. I filled out the form the receptionist handed me, then Momma took it up to her.

She scanned it quickly. "What is the name of your insurance carrier?" she asked.

"We don't have none," Momma answered.

A few of the people in the waiting room looked up from their magazines.

"No insurance?" the pretty young receptionist repeated.

"No," Momma confirmed, looking down at the forest-green carpeting.

"Well, I don't know . . ." the receptionist began. "We normally don't accept patients without insurance coverage."

Now everyone in the waiting room was watching Momma. She stood tall, tugged down her T-shirt, and looked the receptionist dead in the eye. "Look-ee here," she said loudly, "I ain't asking for no free ride. I'll pay whatever it costs."

The receptionist looked down at the form, and her eye found the spot where Momma had put down her occupation. Waitress. No way could Momma afford to pay that doctor.

"Excuse me a moment," the receptionist said, and disappeared from the desk.

"Can we just leave now before I have to be totally humiliated?" I hissed.

"No, we cannot," Momma said. "This doctor is going to see you. And we ain't leaving here until he does." She sat down next to me and folded her arms, looking straight ahead.

Out of the corner of my eye, I saw Kyle look at her with grudging respect.

"I can help pay," he said in a low voice. "I still have some money saved from my summer job—"

"Just shut up!" I interrupted. Kyle offering Momma money was just too awful for words. At the time, it didn't occur to me that he might actually care.

Kyle shook his head, then he quickly looked back down at his magazine.

After about five minutes the receptionist came back. "Ma'am?" she called to Momma. "Just sign your daughter in. The doctor will see her shortly."

The nurse called me about ten minutes later, and took me into a small room, where she weighed me. I was down to 104 pounds. Then she took my blood pressure, took tons of blood, and made me pee into a jar. Every little thing hurt—the blood-pressure cuff, the needle in my arm, just everything. I found that now I could manage to get on and off the toilet by myself, although it took a lot of effort.

After that she ushered me into a different room. I changed into a paper dress and waited endlessly for the doctor, alternatingly freezing and sweating.

I don't know why, but I expected Dr. Major to be some real old guy with white hair. He didn't look to be that old at all. He looked at my chart, introduced himself to me, and sat down. "So, tell me what brought you here," he said.

"Dr. Pinion at school said I needed to come for tests," I told him.

"How are you feeling?"

"Like shi— I mean, I feel awful," I told him, catching myself. "Sort of like I've been run over by a truck," I amended.

"Tell me everything, from when you first started to feel badly," Dr. Major said.

So I did. I told him how I'd been running fevers on and off for weeks, how my joints hurt and felt stiff, how I'd get so exhausted that I felt as if I could just fall over on the spot. Dr. Major nodded, listening attentively to every word. Then he examined me. He looked carefully at my hands, at my feet, and he moved some of my joints around. My fingers, wrists, elbows, knees, and feet hurt the worst.

"You've got some very hot joints," Dr. Major remarked, as he felt my right knee.

"What does that mean?" I asked nervously, wincing even from the slight pressure he was exerting.

"Swollen, tender to the touch," he explained, carefully feeling my left knee.

"Ow!" I yelped, and almost leapt from the examining table. Or would have leapt if I hadn't been so crippled.

"Sorry," Dr. Major said, and ever so gently laid his whole hand over my knee. The heat from his hand felt soothing.

"Okay, why don't you get dressed, and then I'll speak with you and your mother in my office," the doctor said. "Do you need any help?"

"No, I can manage," I told him. Ten minutes later Momma and I were sitting nervously in high-back maroon leather chairs in Dr. Major's office. I scanned the walls while we waited. One side of the room was covered with books, the other side was hung with a half-dozen different diplomas.

Dr. Major bustled into the room and sat behind his large mahogany desk. "I can't tell for certain what's wrong until we get all your test results," he began. "There's certainly a good deal of inflammation in your joints, and you're running a fever. I'm sure you're feeling just generally pretty rotten."

I nodded, waiting for him to continue.

"Based on the symptoms you're exhibiting and

the high rheumatoid factor from the test Dr. Pinion did—I called him and his nurse gave me the results over the phone just now—I believe you probably have rheumatoid arthritis."

"What?" I asked harshly. It had to be some kind of horrible, cosmic joke. Just the night before I'd danced at the Arthritis Telethon. I'd met that little girl, Caroline, and found out that even kids could get arthritis, and I'd watched her shuffling across the room like an old woman.

Just like me. Just like me. Oh, my God, it was just like me.

"What is that?" Momma asked anxiously.

"Arthritis just means inflamed joints," Dr. Major said. "It's a term used for over a hundred different diseases, really."

"With rheumatoid arthritis—or R.A.," Dr. Major continued, "the symptoms are stiff, swollen, painful joints, sometimes a low-grade fever, muscle aches, fatigue, and stiffness after inactivity—especially in the morning."

That sounded like me, all right.

"So, what do I do?" I asked.

"For the moment, not much," Dr. Major said. "First we need the results of your blood tests, which I'll have for you tomorrow. I am going to start you on aspirin therapy."

"Aspirin?" I repeated. "I feel like I'm dying and you're telling me to take an aspirin?"

"Not *an* aspirin," Dr. Major corrected me, "aspirin therapy. You'll take three tablets four times a day to begin. It should help with your pain, but it's also an excellent anti-inflammatory."

"So how long does she take all this aspirin for?" Momma asked skeptically.

"We'll have to wait and see," Dr. Major said. "I'll call you tomorrow with the results of your blood tests, and then I want to see you again in a week."

"When can I go back to school?" I asked.

"When you feel better," the doctor said.

"Well, when will that be?" I asked impatiently.

"I don't know," Dr. Major said honestly. "I hope it will be very soon."

"But every time I've felt better and went back to my regular routine, I just felt sick again!" I exploded. "What am I supposed to do, guess?"

"Well, first of all, as long as you're running a fever and in pain, you need to stay in bed," Dr. Major said. "Rest is the single most valuable thing you can do right now."

"Okay," I agreed grudgingly. "How soon before I can dance again?"

Dr. Major smiled kindly. "I saw your trio—Sizzle, it's called, isn't it?—perform at the Arthritis Telethon last night," he said. "I thought you were terrific."

"Thank you," I said. Momma beamed proudly. "Now, how soon can I dance?"

"The dancing you do is very acrobatic and vigorous," Dr. Major said. "For the time being, I wouldn't recommend that you dance."

"Not dance?"

"Every time you overuse your joints while the synovitis is severe, you'll just increase the inflammation," he explained. "You could risk permanent damage."

"When can I dance again?" I demanded.

"I'm sorry, Amber, I don't have the answer you want," Dr. Major said. "We'll just have to wait and see."

"So, how do you get rid of this disease?" Momma asked.

"Often the body goes into remission for long periods of time—sometimes forever—which means you'll have no symptoms at all," Dr. Major said. "Many people have a bad flare—

131

that's what's happening to you now," he said, nodding at me, "and never have any symptoms again in their entire lives."

"So I'll be cured?" I asked pointedly.

"We can't predict the path of this disease any more than we really know what causes it in the first place," Dr. Major said. "But there is a very good chance that you'll be better soon."

I whipped a strand of hair out of my face angrily. "So, what? I'm supposed to, like, go with the flow and not know when I'll get well or if I'll get well? Is that it?"

"It's difficult, I know—" Dr. Major began.

"No, it's not," I interrupted him. "I'm going to get all better, and I'm going to do it fast. I haven't got time for this."

"Well, a positive attitude is a good thing," Dr. Major agreed, getting up from his chair. "But be gentle with yourself. We have to take this disease one day at a time."

I leaned forward and pushed myself out of my chair, thanked the doctor, and walked slowly towards the door.

"Ah, doctor?" Momma said, twisting the handle to her plastic purse around her fingers. "About your fees . . ."

"I appreciate what Amber did last night to help raise funds for the Arthritis Foundation," Dr. Major said quietly. "I think that can constitute payment."

"Thank you, doctor," Momma said, and we walked back out to the waiting room.

Kyle stood up when he saw me, a question in his eyes.

"Bad news for you," I told him, "I'm going to live."

Kyle's lips got real thin, and he went to get the car from the parking lot.

On the way home, Momma chattered to Kyle about how I was going to be just fine, as long as I rested. She presented this real sugar-coated version of what the doctor had told us. Well, that was okay with me. So far I had licked every obstacle in my life, and I knew I could lick this, too. Of course, there was the little matter of Richmond having seen how I really lived. I was going to have to come up with some kind of great story to get around that. But I'd think of something. And I'd rest long enough to really get better this time, and then everything would be back to normal. No way was I going to let some stupid disease stop me. No way.

The blood tests confirmed everything Dr. Major had suspected, so I had my orders. Rest. And soon, although I still felt tired, I felt somewhat better. I took aspirin—the coated kind that don't kill your stomach—and I rested some more. Sure enough, after a few days I started to feel a lot better. Not normal, but better. Richmond and I talked on the phone every day. He said the sweetest things, but he never offered to come over. I pretended not to care. Momma called the school and told them what was wrong with me, and arranged for Kyle to pick up my homework.

I decided that all I needed to make sure that Richmond was still mine was a good plan. The problem was, I did not do my best work over the phone. I knew that once I was better and Richmond saw me again, once he felt my hot little body in his arms, I could make him forget everything from what my house and my mother looked like to, say, his own name.

Donna called me every other day and told me all the gossip—some kids said I was dying of leukemia; others said I was pregnant. Either way, it was the drama of the year.

So, I felt pretty on top of things, pretty confident, when I got this certain phone call from

Donna. I'd been out of school for a week and a half at that point, and I was feeling better. I'd be stiff in the mornings when I woke up, but a hot shower usually helped a lot. I wasn't usually running a fever anymore, and most of my joints felt considerably better. The worst were my knees and elbows. At night I couldn't find a position to sleep in because just the pressure of the sheet against my elbows or knees was terribly painful. Still, all and all, things were looking up, and I was glad when I picked up the phone and heard Donna. I was hungry to hear all the good gossip, to feel like I was back in the world again.

And it started out that way. First she described the incredibly cute stuff she'd bought at the mall. Then she told me what was going on at school. We had a substitute in geometry who kept giving killer pop quizzes. Kyle and Suzanne Lafayette were still an item. The football team had lost two games in a row. Oh, and by the way, she and Cassie were working every day on a new number for Sizzle that Cassie had choreographed, and just so they could get it right with three dancers, Lindsey Van Owen was dancing with them.

"Oh, cool," I heard myself say. "But tell Cassie I'll be back tomorrow, so Lindsey is out. And we need to perfect the numbers we're already doing before we move on to anything else."

"Well, Cassie says—" Donna began.

"I don't give a flying fishcake what Cassie says," I seethed. Then I took a deep breath. Control. I had to maintain control. "You just tell Cassie to be ready to rehearse tomorrow," I added in a level voice.

"If you're sure you're better," Donna said doubtfully.

"Look, this arthritis thing is no big deal," I insisted. "I'm fine, okay?"

"Okay," Donna agreed, and we hung up.

I called Richmond to tell him the good news— he could pick me up for school the next morning. There was silence on his end of the phone. I could hear him breathing, but he didn't say anything.

"Richmond? Did you hear what I said?" I asked him.

"I heard you," he finally said. "But I . . . uh . . . I didn't know you'd be better, and I kind of promised Cassie I'd give her a ride."

"Cassie Stewart?" I asked incredulously.

"It's not how it looks," he said quickly. "I have to go in early for a football drill, and Cassie said she needed to go in early to work on some choreography thing."

"It happens to be *my* choreography thing," I snapped, "and I need to get there early, too."

"Well, Cassie lives all the way on the other side of town from you," Richmond said. "If I pick you both up I'll have to leave my house an hour early."

"So don't pick her up," I said, my voice dripping icicles.

"But I already gave my word," he said.

"What are you, a boy scout or my boyfriend?" I demanded. "*Un*give it, Richie. That is, if you ever want to be with me again."

Richmond sighed. "Okay," he finally agreed. "I'll be at your house tomorrow morning at seven-thirty."

I exhaled. I'd won this round. "Great, sugar," I purred. Then I added a few comments guaranteed to get him hot and bothered, and I said good-bye.

"Baby?" Momma called as she walked in the front door. "I picked up the mail, and look!" She handed me a buff-colored envelope with a picture of Ed McMahon in the corner, underneath which was the return address for *Star Search*.

I sat in the nearest chair, and with trembling fingers I tore open the envelope and quickly scanned the letter.

"Dear Ms. Harkin," it read, "Congratulations! We have viewed your videotape, and your trio, Sizzle, has been selected to perform in the dance competition of *Star Search . . .*"

"Momma?" I whispered, looking up at her.

"Yes, baby?"

"We're in! We're in!"

Then Momma screamed and I screamed and I would have jumped around the room with joy if I could have, only my knees were too swollen and stiff for me to do any jumping.

Or any dancing.

CHAPTER ELEVEN

"Amber-Lynn?" Momma asked haltingly. "What about your illness?"

"I'm better!" I told her. "You know I'm better."

"I know, baby, but just last week Dr. Major told you that there was still too much inflammation in your knees for you to dance."

"Well, that was then; this is now," I snapped. "Besides, I'm inside my body; he isn't. I think I know how I feel."

"Does it say when ya'll need to be to Los Angeles?" Momma asked.

"In ten days. Just think how much better I'll be in ten days!"

"Well, I'm just so proud of you, baby," Momma said, giving me a fierce hug. "I always told you, you could do anything you set your mind to, and dang if you haven't proved me right."

"Thanks, Momma," I said, hugging her back. It was true—she really had always believed in me. For just one second I wondered about my father—whoever he was. *Too bad you missed knowing me, sucker,* I told him fiercely in my head. *I'm gonna be somebody.*

It's a funny thing about prayer.

Sometimes on Sundays Momma and I would go to the Baptist church that's just down the road from us, and we'd sit there through the service, through Reverend Earl's sermon, and usually I spent the time going over dance steps in my mind, or looking at the tacky outfits some of the women were wearing and wondering how they could possibly go out of the house looking like that. I don't recall that I ever actually prayed there.

But there I was, that night before I went back to school, knowing we'd been picked for *Star Search,* knowing that my knees hurt when I walked, forget what they'd feel like when I tried to dance the next day, and once again I found myself praying as hard as I could. *Please God,* I prayed, *let me be able to dance. Please take away this illness and make me well, and I'll never ask for another thing as long as I live.*

I was into making deals, you see. And I guess it won't surprise you to know that once again my prayers were not answered.

I woke up early, and reached down to feel my knees. They felt hot and spongy, and it hurt if I pressed on them. I hobbled into the shower, and as usual the hot water helped loosen me up. Then I sat on my bed with my athletic tape and I taped my knees as if I were going into combat. I'd heard about ballet dancers who did pointe work on broken ankles; they just taped them and went on. Well, I figured arthritis couldn't possibly be as bad as a broken ankle. I pulled on some black leggings, a little lacy black bra, my zip-up-the-front leotard, and my Nikes, threw some jeans and a shirt for later into a bag, and was waiting in front when Richmond drove up.

"Hey, babe," he said, giving me a perfunctory kiss. He looked nervous and guilty. How much was really going on between him and Cassie? I couldn't lose Richmond to that witch. I just refused to let it happen.

"I'm back in action," I told him, and tickled his

chin with the end of my hair as if I didn't have a care in the world.

"Great!" he said, gunning the car down the street. He wouldn't quite look me in the eye, even at the red lights.

"So, what's shakin'?" I asked.

"Oh, you know, same old same old," he said, his eyes on the road. "We lost that big away game."

"You told me that on the phone," I reminded him.

"Oh, right. Well, Suzanne Lafayette had a party afterwards, but everyone was feeling kind of punk."

This was news. No one had told me that Richmond's ex had had a party. Maybe I was worrying about Cassie for nothing. Maybe it was Suzanne.

"Did you dance with her?"

"I don't remember," Richmond said. "Anyway, like I said, I was in a piss-poor mood on account of the game and all."

"Did you dance with Cassie?"

"What is this, the third degree?" Richmond asked me defensively.

Something was definitely wrong. My magic

wasn't working. I was losing my powers over him.

Drastic measures were in order.

"Pull down that street!" I yelled suddenly, pointing to a little side street coming up on the right.

"Why—?"

"Just do it!" I told him.

He turned the wheel sharply, but bitched as he did it. "Amber, what are we doing?"

"There's something up here I've just got to show you!" I said urgently. "Okay, turn down this dirt road," I instructed him. We were on a deserted street running parallel to a creek. "Stop."

He did. "Amber, there's nothing to see here," he said with disgust.

"Yes, there is," I said. I turned to face him, then I slowly unzipped my leotard, all the way to the waist.

"Amber, Lord . . ." he breathed, mesmerized by his first glimpse of bodacious me clad only in a sexy brassiere.

"I missed you," I whispered.

"I . . . I . . ." he stammered, then he gulped hard. "I have to get to football drill."

"Uh huh," I agreed, and then, without taking

my eyes from his eyes, I just reached down and flicked the little clasp on the front of my bra. It sprang open. And there were my naked breasts gleaming in the morning sunlight for Richmond Remington the Third to adore.

Only he didn't.

"Jesus and Mary, cover yourself," he said harshly, a look of disgust on his face.

I sat there a second, unable to move.

"Come on, Amber." He reached over and kind of pulled my clothes around me, then he looked away as I hurriedly re-fastened my clothes. Without a word, he started the car and drove all the way to school. I didn't say anything when I got out of the car, either. I just slammed the door and ran.

Tramp. Slut. Just like your mother.

Oh, God. How could I have done that?

Fortunately the ladies' room was empty when I burst through the door. My knees were throbbing and swelling in their bandages. Everything hurt. I was already exhausted, sweaty, a mess. I stared at my face in the mirror—ugly, red from exertion and illness and humiliation.

"I hate you," I whispered into the mirror.

Tramp. Slut. Just like your mother.

I heard the door to the john opening, and like a flash I was in one of the stalls so no one could see me.

"I'm not kidding," one girl said. "He told Cassie and Cassie told me. He said it was disgusting, filthy, with actual holes in the walls!" I was pretty sure I recognized her voice—Brittany Schaeffer, a rich, stuck-up friend of Cassie's who was in my English class.

"Unbelievable!" the other girl said. "Can I borrow your blush?"

"Oh, and listen to this," the first girl said. "It was *infested*. I mean it!"

"With *bugs*?" the second girl shrieked.

"That's what Cassie said. And her mother is, like, this hooker or something!"

"Well, that doesn't surprise me. Cassie says she's done it with practically every guy in the junior class. Do we have time for a cigarette?"

"I've got to go get those psych notes from Amy. God, my hair looks like road kill today."

I heard them both leave and then I came out of the stall. They were talking about me. Spreading vicious lies about me. My house might be a shack, but we did not have bugs. I spent half my life cleaning just to make sure we didn't. Cassie was just trying to ruin me. Richmond was in on it. Well, I wasn't going to roll over and die. I had something those witches didn't have. Talent. Everyone was going to sing a different tune when Sizzle won *Star Search*.

I popped some extra aspirin and headed for the gym, where I was supposed to meet Donna and Cassie. I vowed to put everything else out of my mind except Sizzle and *Star Search*. Soon they'd all be singing a different tune. And when I was rich and famous and a guest on the *Arsenio* show, I'd mention them by name but only to say what hateful, ugly lowlifes they were.

When I got to the gym Cassie was already there doing warm-up stretches. She looked extremely cool and confident in a white leotard with the stomach part cut out, showing her perfectly muscled, tanned abdomen. Big deal. My stomach looked just like that, too, but at the moment mine was covered with slimy sweat from the simple exertion of walking to the gym.

Cassie flipped her perfect red hair out of her eye and sauntered over to me. "Hi. Glad to see you're better."

Yeah, I bet. "Thanks," I said, and began to warm up. "Where's Donna?"

"I'm here!" Donna called, running into the gym. "I'm so glad to see you!" she said, giving me a hug, as if she really meant it.

I tried not to wince, even though all my joints hurt when she hugged me. "Ya'll, I have news," I said significantly. I pulled the letter from *Star Search* out of my gym bag and waved it slowly in the air in front of their faces.

"Oh, my God!" Donna screamed. "Is that what I think it is?"

"If you think it's the letter picking us to be on *Star Search,* it is," I said with a triumphant smile.

"Eeeeeeeeek!" Donna screamed. "We did it! We really did it! Now my parents have to actually come through!"

She was referring to the deal we'd made with her parents. They said that if we actually got picked to be on *Star Search* they'd pay for our trip out to Los Angeles. Donna and I had talked about it many times—they'd never seen Sizzle dance, and clearly they believed they'd never really have to fulfill this little deal. But, as Donna said, they could certainly afford it, so it was no big deal.

Donna saw Bobby Pratt across the gym, stretching out before going out to the football field and gave a triumphant hoot. "We're gonna be on *Star Search!*" she screamed to him.

Cassie folded her arms and looked me over critically. "You ready for that?"

"It's two weeks away," I told her, "and yes, I'm ready."

"You look kind of . . . well, awful, if you don't mind my telling you what I really think," Cassie said innocently.

"I don't mind," I replied, "because I couldn't care less what you really think or what you say or who you say it to," I added pointedly.

"I have no idea what you're talking about," Cassie said.

"Oh, I think you do," I said, my eyes narrowing. "But I just take it from the source—trash talking trash."

Cassie giggled musically. "Well, that's amusing, coming from you."

"Look, I'm not sinking to your level," I told her. "All I care about is your dancing. If you screw up, you're out."

"And if you screw up, you're out," she replied in a cold voice.

"You can't do that; it's my group!" I exclaimed.

"Prove it," she said, looking me over again. Then she turned her back on me and began stretching her hamstrings.

She's not getting to you. She cannot get to you, I chanted to myself, taking a deep breath. I looked around for Donna. She was surrounded by half the football team and a few girls who had been hanging around flirting with the guys on the team—including Richmond. "Donna!" I called to her irritably. "Let's get to work!"

The crowd crossed the gym with Donna. "Tell them!" Donna insisted. "Show them the letter from Ed McMahon!"

I looked away from Richmond, and noticed Brittany Schaeffer in the crowd, wearing an outfit worth more than my entire wardrobe. "It's true," I told them, pulling the letter out of my gym bag. I gave Brittany a nasty little smile. "Now, if ya'll don't mind, we're going to rehearse, because we intend to win." I slipped a cassette into the cassette player. "We'll start with 'Buff Enough,'" I told Cassie and Donna. "I'm assuming you did your stretches at home."

The crowd moved back to watch us rehearse, obviously all really excited. We weren't just some Nashville dance act now; we were going national on prime time. The whole country was about to see us. Were we really that good? Could it really happen? There was a buzz of expectation in the crowd, but I ignored it and held my body still, waiting on the balls of my feet for the introductory bars of our music. *Please let me do this, God,* I prayed. *I have to do this. I have to show them.*

There it was, the wailing guitars and the pulsing drum coming in for four, and then I began to move to the music. I didn't feel anything; I refused to feel anything. I just let the music carry me, lift me through the air. Yes! I could do it! I could dance! A double spin with my head thrown back, my hair whipping into my face. *Take that, Richmond!* I screamed triumphantly in my head. *Take that, you rich bitches!*

We weren't even halfway through the number and I was gasping for breath. It didn't matter. I pushed myself, sucking extra air into my lungs. Now came the double spin into the lunge on the left knee. As I landed on my left leg, I felt a terrible *ping* of pain so excruciating I would have fallen over, but the next move favored my right leg and I was able to go on. Swooping down from the next lift, I felt the pain in both knees and tears came to my eyes. I wouldn't stop dancing. Now I couldn't breathe; not enough air could possibly get into my body through those tiny passages, my nose, my mouth, and the pain shot through my legs, my arms, my whole body, screaming, screaming, but I wouldn't stop, no matter what. Down into the one-handed push-ups, and then it happened. My body went down on the floor, inert, my arm unable to hold me. I felt a hush go through that crowd, that crowd just waiting for me to fall, and I lay there on the floor of the gym, sobbing into my arms while they all watched.

CHAPTER TWELVE

An ambulance came and took me to St. Thomas Hospital, where they admitted me and put me on an intravenous drip of a steroid drug called prednisone. The school called Momma, and Kayla brought her over to the hospital. She showed up with pink foam rubber curlers in her hair, wearing a pair of rubber flip-flops on her bare feet. She was makeup-less except for a slash of red lipstick that she'd obviously put on with a shaking hand, since it extended around her lip line at certain points. Someone came in and took a ton of my blood, then Dr. Major had Momma go into the hall while he examined me.

"You danced, huh?" he said softly, sitting down next to my hospital bed.

"I had to," I whispered fiercely. "You wouldn't understand."

"Maybe not," he agreed. "I know this is hard for you, but you've got to accept a certain truth right now. You cannot dance. You are risking permanent and serious crippling."

I gulped hard. "It could go away, into remission, though, right?" I said.

"It could," he agreed. "But the worse the flare and the longer it lasts, the worse the odds are of that happening."

"Well, it has to happen," I insisted flatly.

Dr. Major sighed, then he called Momma back into the room. "The prednisone drip should help with her pain," he told me, "but it's not something I want her on long-term."

"Why not?" I asked, seeing only a lifeline. "If the pain would go away, I could dance."

"First of all, it's a dangerous drug with very serious side effects," Dr. Major said. "Second of all, it doesn't deal with the disease, it only masks the symptoms. I'll be steadily lowering your dose while you're here. I absolutely don't want you on prednisone any longer than you need to be."

"Great," I snorted.

"I'm going to start you on stronger anti-inflammatories," Dr. Major continued, "which you'll take twice a day. And I'd like to try gold injections."

"Gold injections?" Momma repeated nervously. "You shoot gold into her?"

"That's right," Dr. Major said. "We'll start with weekly injections, done in my office. At the same time I'll do a blood test and you'll give me a urine sample so we're sure you're not having any side effects."

"Will it make me well?" I demanded.

"It has a good effect on about three-quarters of the patients who try it," the doctor said.

"Then I'll do it," I announced. "Start it now."

"Like what side effects?" Momma asked, fiddling anxiously with one of her curlers.

"It's a serious therapy to deal with a serious disease," Dr. Major said. "Some people develop rashes or sores in the mouth."

"That's nothing," I said.

"It's not nothing," Dr. Major corrected me. "It can mean the drug is becoming toxic for you. And a certain small percentage of patients develop more serious side effects, which is what we have to watch for—kidney problems or bone-marrow suppression."

"That won't happen to me," I stated.

"Also, it takes about six months before you'll get the full prophylactic effects," the doctor said, "though you may feel some improvement in three or four."

"Six months?" I repeated. "It can't take six months. I have to dance on *Star Search* in two weeks."

"Amber, I can't say this any other way," Dr. Major began sternly. "You cannot dance in two weeks. You cannot dance in two months. I do not know if you will ever be able to dance again."

"But . . . but I have to . . ." I faltered.

"I'm sorry, Amber," Dr. Major said gently. "This is beyond your control." He patted my hand and walked out.

"I want another doctor," I told my mother.

"Amber, honey, he's a very good doctor, famous even . . ."

"I don't care!" I yelled. "What the hell does he know?"

"He knows, baby," Momma said. "And you have to listen to him."

"I don't have to do anything!" I yelled. "And how could you show up here with rollers in your hair? Don't you have any pride?"

Momma self-consciously touched one pink sponge roller and then her hand fluttered around her face. "Oh, Lordie, I must look a sight. I just forgot. I didn't think, I just ran out the door."

I turned my head to the wall, away from her injured, embarrassed face. I didn't want to care about anyone or anything. Ever.

I went home the next day feeling like I was a hundred years old. Everything hurt so much, it was hard for me to believe I wasn't dying. At Dr. Major's suggestion Momma bought me a cane, which would have made it possible for me to get around the house a little. I hated that cane so much that I pretty much refused to use it, which pretty much meant I couldn't walk. It hardly mattered, since most of the time I didn't have the energy to do more than sleep. Momma and Kayla took turns looking after me, making me soup, fluffing my pillows, and telling me dirty jokes. For five days no one else came over and the phone didn't ring. Finally, late on the first afternoon that Momma and Kayla actually left me alone, Donna called.

"Hey, Amber!" came that perky voice over the phone.

"Gee, long time no hear," I said sarcastically.

"Well, I just kept meaning to call . . ." Donna began.

"Forget it. It doesn't matter."

"So . . . how are you feeling?" she asked.

"Fine," I replied, like the big liar I am. Even holding the phone hurt.

"Does that mean you're coming back to school?"

"No, I'm dropping out to become a stripper," I told her sarcastically. "Of course I'm coming back to school."

"Oh, good. But, um . . . what about Sizzle?" she asked.

"I'll be fine in a few days," I told her. "We'll just rehearse extra hard."

"Are you sure?"

"Donna Martin, are you hard of hearing?" I yelled. "I just told you I'm fine!"

"Well, I kind of heard differently," she said tentatively.

"What did you kind of hear?" I asked.

"Well, the school nurse told Ms. Finch, the gym teacher, that you couldn't dance anymore," Donna began. "Ms. Finch gave us a whole talk about you and health and nutrition before cheerleading practice yesterday."

"Oh, big deal," I tossed off, clutching the phone more tightly. "She doesn't know what she's talking about. She's just jealous because her thighs look like ham hocks."

It was then that I heard a snort, a snort I knew didn't belong to Donna. "Who else is on this phone?" I demanded.

"I am," came Cassie's voice, cool as you please.

"Well, thank you so much for letting me know," I said.

Cassie didn't even bother to make excuses. "Amber, Donna and I don't think Sizzle should pass up this opportunity because you're sick," she said.

"I just told you—" I began.

"Look, you can't fool me," Cassie said. "My aunt has rheumatoid arthritis. She's had it for years. She walks with a cane—that is, when she can walk at all."

"I don't have it that badly," I protested.

"Yes, you do," Cassie said. "I saw you. You could hardly walk. You can't dance."

"I can!" I insisted, but Cassie ignored me.

"I know you don't want your friends to miss this opportunity. So Donna and I voted to ask

Lindsey Van Owen to join Sizzle, and Lindsey said yes."

"It's only temporary," Donna whined, her voice pleading with me not to be angry. "Until you're better, Amber."

"We have our first rehearsal in an hour," Cassie continued. "We just wanted to let you know."

"Amber?" Donna called. "Say something!"

"Both of you can go to hell!" is what I said, and I slammed the phone down as hard as I could. It was too horrible, beyond words. My whole body was shaking. Sizzle was mine! They couldn't do it! I had to prove I could dance! That would show them! I had to show up at the Sizzle rehearsal.

I threw the covers off of me, which hurt my wrist terribly, then I pivoted my legs over the side of the bed. Slowly, I pushed myself into a standing position, my ankles and knees screaming at supporting my weight. I grabbed for my cane, which was leaning in the corner, and then like Frankenstein I shuffled my feet towards the bathroom, determined to make it to the shower.

The hot water loosened me up like it usually did, but still when I got out of the shower I found I couldn't go more than two steps without the cane. I hobbled back into the bedroom and threw on some dance clothes, sticking my hair up on my head in a big ponytail. Then I quickly put some make-up on my face—lipstick, mascara, and blush. It was awkward, since I could barely bend my elbow enough to bring my hand to my face. I stood up and limped around some more. I told myself it wasn't so different from feeling stiff when I danced too hard without warming up. All I really needed was to stretch out my muscles and I'd be fine. I bent down to touch my toes, and it hurt. God, it hurt so much. But I couldn't pay any attention to that. I began to do my warm-up stretches, staring with total concentration at a crack in the wall. Nothing existed except me and pain. I didn't care. I forced myself to walk to the phone without using my cane, and I dialed Kyle's number, praying he and his mother's car were both home.

"Yeah?" came Kyle's voice.

"I need a favor," I told him without preamble, knowing he'd recognize my voice. "I need a ride to The Gym."

"Come on, Amber . . ." he chided me softly.

"I have to go," I said urgently. "I mean it. If

you won't drive me, I'll find some other way to get there. I'll hitch if I have to."

Silence.

"Kyle?"

"I'll come over and we'll talk," he finally said. "I'll bring you some ice cream."

"I don't want your damn ice cream!" I screamed. "Just forget it!" I slammed down the phone. What ever made me think that Kyle would come through for me? It didn't matter. None of them mattered. I would just have to depend on myself. I limped over to where I'd dropped my gym bag and threw it over my shoulder, which sent waves of pain shooting through my collar bone. Then I picked up my cane and headed out the door.

I limped down to the corner where there was a convenience store, so exhausted by the effort I could barely stand. Leaning heavily on the cane, I stuck out my thumb, ready to hitch a ride with the first car that stopped. After about ten minutes, an old car full of guys I didn't know screeched to a halt in front of me.

"Hey, beautiful," the blond-haired guy on the passenger side called to me out his window. "You sprain your ankle or something?"

"Yeah," I replied, flashing him my best smile. "Are ya'll heading towards Twenty-first Avenue South? I need to get to The Gym."

"Now, how you gonna work out with your ankle all messed up, sweet thang?" a guy asked from the back seat.

"I'd like to give you a workout, sugar," the blond in the front seat told me, wiggling his eyebrows. "Get in." He opened the car door and stared at me meaningfully.

Before I could answer, another old car swerved around the car full of guys and came to a screeching halt. Someone slid over to the passenger side and pushed the door open. It was Kyle.

I limped away from the car full of boys, who hooted and hollered at me as I made my way slowly to Kyle's car. I climbed in and sat down next to him without a word. He started driving towards The Gym.

"Thanks," I finally mumbled. He stared straight ahead and didn't say a word. "They're trying to replace me in Sizzle," I finally told him. "I've got to stop them."

He stopped at a red light and looked at me for the first time. "How you plannin' on doing that?"

"I'm going to dance."

"I know you're taking psych this year," Kyle said. "Didn't you ever hear of denial?"

"Meaning you think I'm refusing to see reality," I translated. "Kyle, surely you know by now. I create my own reality."

Kyle got a look of disgust on his face and shook his head. He didn't say another word until he pulled up in front of The Gym.

"Thanks," I said, slowly maneuvering myself out of his car. He shook his head at me again and varoomed off down the street.

Just the small amount of sitting still in the car had caused me to stiffen up again. The first few steps I took were total misery. I figured if I leaned heavily on my cane until I actually got inside, it would help save my energy. *I can do this,* I told myself, inching my way towards the front door. *It's simply mind over matter. I create my own reality.*

I pulled the front door open and cried out at the pain that went pounding through my fingers. Once inside the familiar building, I took a deep breath, straightened up, and shoved the cane into the corner, behind an umbrella stand. The first person who saw me was Crater.

"Amber-Lynn?" he asked, sounding incredulous. "Well, hog-tie me to a tadpole, you're a sight for sore eyes!" He enveloped me in a bear hug that hurt so much I cried out involuntarily.

"Hey, Crater," I finally managed, trying hard not to let my lips tremble with the pain. "I understand we've got a Sizzle rehearsal going on."

"Well, yeah," Crater replied, looking troubled. "Did you come to watch?"

I stood as tall as I could and put my shoulders back. "I came to dance," I said with dignity.

"But, but . . ." Crater stammered.

"But what?" I challanged him.

"Sweet pea, you don't look so hot. It looks like a good wind could blow you over," he said apologetically. "Maybe you'd better sit down." He reached out for me, but I moved away.

"I'm going to rehearsal," I told him. Then, concentrating all my effort on not limping, I headed slowly to the back room.

The music to "Buff Enough" grew louder as I made my way down the corridor. By the time I got to the door outside the back room, I was dripping with sweat and pasty-faced with exhaustion. My left knee was throbbing with pain. Everything hurt. I leaned against the wall, panting with exhaustion, barely able to stand. I put my cheek against the cool glass picture window and looked into the room.

There were Donna and Cassie and Lindsey dancing to "Buff Enough." I watched them as they spun and dipped and leaped through the air, as they fell into the one-handed push-ups, hanging tough, looking fine. I watched them go into the big finish, and then I watched Richmond Remington the Third, who was standing in the corner, clap and whistle, and run over to Cassie and wrap his arms around her.

The glass grew slick from my tears, my cheek slid down until I sank all the way down to the floor. I knew then. I finally, really faced it. I would never be able to dance again.

"Amber?"

I looked up through my tears at Kyle, standing there over me. I couldn't speak. Kyle didn't say anything, either. He just knelt down and carefully picked me up, and he carried me all the way out to his car. I heard Crater mumble "here" and hand Kyle my cane when we went past the front desk, and I knew all those perfect-looking girls in their sexy little workout outfits were staring at me, but I kept my face buried in Kyle's chest. He set me carefully down in the front seat, then went around to his side, got in, and started the car.

"That was a damn stupid thing to do," Kyle finally said in a gruff voice. "Don't you think I have anything better to do than to chase after you?"

I didn't answer him. I just stared out the window.

"I came back to check that you were all right," he groused. "I swear, girl, sometimes you are dumb as a box of rocks."

He went on bitching at me, but I just tuned him out. It didn't matter what he said. Nothing mattered. It was as if his voice was coming at me from far, far away. He kept up this monologue, about how I had to be more mature, how I had to take care of myself now, be responsible. It started to rain. I smiled out at the rain drops. Everything would be okay now.

Because I had a plan.

I didn't protest when Kyle stopped in front of my house and carried me inside. He set me down on my bed and stood over me. "Do I need to stay here and look after you?" he asked me, folding his arms in front of himself.

"No," I replied sweetly. "Thanks for your help."

Kyle got a weird look on his face. "You sure?"

"I'm fine," I assured him. "You were right all along. I don't know what I was thinking."

"Maybe I'd better stay . . ." Kyle began.

"No, I'm just going to go to sleep. You don't need to watch me sleep."

"Are you sure?" he asked again, a skeptical scowl on his face.

"Absolutely," I insisted. "You're sweet to worry." I smiled at him and snuggled down into my pillow. "You can run along."

He looked undecided for a moment, then he reached down and pushed a loose strand of hair off my face. And then he was gone.

As soon as I heard the door slam behind him, I got up and grabbed my cane, then I limped into the bathroom. I opened the medicine cabinet, and there it was. A bottle of tranquilizers some doctor at the free clinic had prescribed for Momma about a year ago, when she got so nervous after J.J. gave her a black eye and a sprained shoulder one night. I opened the bottle and stared at the pills. It was almost full—Momma had hated the spacy way they'd made her feel, so she'd quit taking them after a couple of days.

I limped to the refrigerator and got out some lemonade, poured a glass, and carried it into the bedroom. I tried to think about who would care if I was dead. No one, really. Not Donna, who was supposed to be my best friend. Not Richmond, obviously. Not Kyle, who would certainly rather spend his time with the lovely Suzanne Lafayette. Not even Crater, who it seemed only had a crush on me so long as I was healthy and sexy. Well, who could blame him?

Slut. Tramp. Just like your mother.

Momma. There was Momma to think about. Should I leave her a note? Yes, that would be good. I didn't want Momma to feel too badly about everything. Once I was gone, though, it would be so much easier for her to be with J.J. Everything would be easier, really. And she'd get over feeling sad soon enough. I pulled a piece of notebook paper out of my looseleaf.

"Dear Momma," I wrote, "Please don't feel badly about this. You've been a wonderful mother but I haven't been a wonderful daughter. I can't dance anymore. I'm nothing and I want to die. Love, Amber."

I propped the paper up on the dresser, right next to an old picture of Madonna I had cut out of a magazine years before. Then I took the twelve Swatch watches out of my drawer and dropped them one by one into the white plastic wastepaper basket. They made kind of a pretty still life, lying there like that. I poured the pills into my hand, put them in my mouth, and swallowed the entire glass of lemonade. I looked at the picture of Madonna again and smiled. Surely she would do the exact same thing if she were in my position.

Then I lay down and waited to die.

CHAPTER THIRTEEN

Kyle saved my life, and I hated him for it.

He came back about an hour after he dropped me off, and there I was passed out, half-dead. He called the ambulance, and it came and took me to St. Thomas Hospital, where they pumped my stomach, and so I lived. I don't remember any of this, of course. I was completely out of it. Some people have asked me what it felt like to almost die, and the truth is I don't remember. I just remember going to sleep, and then nothing. Nothing, that is, until I woke up in the hospital with this tube down my throat and an ugly old nurse watching my every breath. When she saw my eyes were open she ran and got the doctor—some resident with bad breath and hair sticking out of his left nostril—then they finally removed that god-awful tube I was gagging on, and then they let Momma in.

"Baby?" Momma whispered, tiptoeing over to my bed.

I thought that all I felt was angry, but when I saw her face I started to cry. "I'm sorry," I croaked out. It hurt like the devil to talk.

"I just thank God you're okay," she said with a tremulous smile. "I know you didn't really want to die, baby."

"Yes, Momma, I did," I whispered. Then I closed my eyes so that I wouldn't have to see her tortured face.

Well, of course they made me stay in the hospital for a while, only they transferred me to the you-tried-to-kill-yourself wing with the other nut cases. They cut off my visitors—too disturbing, they said—and I had to see a psychiatrist. Her name was Dr. Nancy Pigeon, and just like a pigeon she had a big ole chest and little tiny stick legs, beady eyes, and a beaky sort of nose.

"Well, Amber, would you like to talk about it, hmmmm?" she asked me as we sat in her beige-on-beige office.

"No," I told her, which I thought deserved points for honesty.

"You tried to kill yourself," she said, her beady eyes drilling holes into my head.

"Aren't you the mental giant," I marveled.

This sort of conversation went on for a few days, until she gave up on me and I got switched to Elaine Wolstein. She was a doctor, too, although she looked like someone's grandmother—and she said I could call her Elaine if she could call me Amber. She had brown, graying hair that she wore in a bun and wore a Jewish star around her neck. She had no fashion sense but a great smile. I started to like her in spite of my resolutions not to.

"Let's look at this pragmatically," she told me at our first session. "If you don't talk, you don't get released, and you probably don't get better. If you talk, you'll get out of here and I hope, eventually, you'll be in less pain."

That made sense. The getting out part, anyway. Because, you see, I wasn't in any pain. I was completely numb and cut off from my feelings, so I really didn't have any pain at all. And I did want to get out. Badly.

Because that would be the only way I could try to kill myself again. This time I'd succeed.

Ha. I bet you didn't expect that. You thought I'd wake up and be so sorry and want to live. Well, it didn't happen that way. I woke up and my joints hurt and I had to use a cane to get down the hall of the damn hospital like some old lady and I wanted to die more than ever.

So, I started talking to Elaine. I told her that I was a dancer who couldn't ever dance again. I told her that was all I cared about in the world. I planned to make it just a simple recitation of facts, only there I was in her office crying and screaming and I couldn't stop for a long, long time.

"Of course you're sad, Amber," she told me. "You're in mourning." Something about the way she said it made me cry all over again. And something about her and her dumpy body and ugly print dresses and kind, smart eyes made me believe that she understood. That was it. Someone—the me I had been, the me I could've been, the only me I wanted to be—had died.

We talked every day, and slowly I stopped feeling like I wanted to die. On the other hand, I wasn't convinced I wanted to live, either. But Elaine asked me would I try to kill myself again and I honestly told her no. A few days after that she said I could have visitors again if I wanted to, and that's when Kyle came to visit.

"I hate daisies," I told him when he walked in carrying a semiwilted cone of them wrapped in purple paper.

"Well, give them to someone who likes them, then," he said, throwing them on the nightstand. My roommate, Barbi (who drew a happy face to dot the "i" in her name), a recovering anorexic who giggled uncontrollably whenever a reasonably cute guy was in the vicinity, began to giggle and made a grab for the flowers.

"How about if you go put them in water and take a really long time," I suggested.

She took the hint, giggled, and left the room.

"I see your mouth has recovered," Kyle observed.

"I'm not bucking for sainthood," I snapped at him.

He sat in an ugly orange plastic chair and stared at the ceiling as if he was asking God for help in dealing with me.

"So how do you feel?" he finally asked me.

I shrugged petulantly.

"Do you want me to start bringing you your homework?" he asked.

I shrugged again.

"God, Amber-Lynn, sometimes I'd like to slap you silly!" he exploded.

"I don't think you're supposed to talk that way to a nut case," I reminded him. "Besides, I'm pissed at you."

"For what?" he asked incredulously. "Saving your life?"

"Yes!" I yelled. "No one asked you to come swooping in to save the day!"

"Well, excuse me for caring!" Kyle jumped out of his seat and took a step towards me.

"Oh, get off it, Kyle!" I screamed, staring him down. "You don't give a rat's ass about me!"

"Oh, I don't," Kyle mocked. "You know me better than I know me, huh?"

"Yes! I do!" I assured him.

"So, I suppose I'm not in love with you, then!" he challenged me.

"Ha!" I barked.

"I suppose I haven't always been in love with you, my whole life!" he yelled. He stared at me a moment, tears coming to his eyes. "I suppose that when I saw you lying there, and I thought you were dead, that I didn't want to die, too," he continued, his voice softer now, "because I couldn't imagine living in a world that you weren't in."

For once in my life, I was speechless.

"But, but, you don't even like me . . ." I stammered. "You called me a slut and a tramp."

"That was *years* ago, Amber," Kyle said slowly, pain etched across his face. "I was a stupid kid. And I was jealous because you were with that other guy instead of me."

"But . . . you never told me that," I said, tears falling down my face. "I thought you hated me."

"Amber, I love you."

Then he took two steps towards me and I was in his arms. It was like coming home. I cried my mascara off onto his white T-shirt while he held me. Then I moved away and punched him hard in the arm.

"Ow! What the hell was that for?"

"For never apologizing! For letting me think all these years that you hated me!"

"I apologize," Kyle said, rubbing his arm. "So when do you get out of here?"

"I kind of like it here," I said, sitting down on the bed.

"Seriously, Amber-Lynn."

I picked some lint off the white chenille bedspread. "I can't go back and face all those kids," I whispered.

"Yes, you can," Kyle assured me.

"No, I really can't," I said. "Cassie spread all these rumors about me, and everyone saw me fall on my face in the gym, and Sizzle is going on without me. I can't face them! I'll transfer to a different high school."

Kyle came and sat next to me on the bed. He put his arm around me and gently stroked some hair off my face. "I think they've already done about everything terrible they can do to you, babe," he pointed out. "But if you don't go back and face them, then they win."

"Fine, they win, then," I said bluntly.

"I know you better than that," Kyle said quietly.

"Do you?" I said, staring at him. "Go stand by the door."

"What for?"

"Just do it!" I told him. Then I pushed myself

up off the bed and grabbed my cane. Then slowly, I limped across the room to him. "This is how I walk now, Kyle," I whispered. "Some days I feel like I can barely get out of bed. My knees hurt so bad that just touching them makes me cry. I get exhausted walking across a room. Do you really think I can go back and win?" I turned around and limped back to the bed, as much to hide my tears from him as for any other reason.

"Will it get better?" he asked me.

"Maybe yes, maybe no," I told him. "I'm getting these shots now—gold injections—and maybe in a few months it'll help. If not Dr. Major says he'll try a different drug."

"It sucks," Kyle said.

"Don't you dare feel sorry for me," I warned him.

"Why should I? Seems to me you're doing a good enough job feeling sorry for yourself for the both of us," Kyle said, and came back over to the bed.

"Should I be jumping for joy?" I demanded. "Wait, that's a silly question, because I can't jump! I can't dance! I can barely walk."

Kyle didn't say a word.

"What am I supposed to do if I can't dance?" I asked him.

"I don't know," he finally said.

"What would you do if you couldn't write songs anymore? How would you feel if you had to give up your dream?"

"About as low as you do, I reckon," Kyle admitted. "But then I'd up and find me a new dream."

"Just like that?" I demanded acidly.

"No, I guess it would take time and work," Kyle said carefully, "but that's what I'd do."

"It's easy to be noble when it's only theoretical," I said bitterly. "You don't know *how* you'd be."

"You're right," he agreed, and tenderly drew his knuckles across my cheek. "But Amber, you've already faced a lot of hard things in your life. You can face this, too."

"I don't know who I am now," I whispered.

"Same smart, gorgeous, wonderful, ornery woman you were before," Kyle said, "only you can't dance. You'll find another dream."

I stared down at my tender, swollen hands. "You don't think I'm ugly now?" I gulped out. "I feel so ugly . . ."

"Amber-Lynn, you're a princess," he told me. Then he gently turned my face to his, and he kissed me.

And I didn't feel ugly anymore.

"Wh . . . what about Suzanne?" I asked him, wiping the tears from my face.

"I broke up with her last week," Kyle said. "I knew I had to face what was really going on between you and me, and I knew I had to be free to do it."

I gave him an arched look. "Well, weren't you cocky!"

"What other kind of guy do you think could handle you?" he said with a laugh.

I took his hand and held it lightly. He was careful not to put too much pressure on my swollen joints. "I still don't know how I'm going to face them, Kyle."

"You can do it," Kyle told me. "You have more guts in your little finger than those fools have in their entire anatomy. And I'll be with you, every step of the way."

I smiled at him. God, he looked so beautiful. "Kyle," I wondered aloud. "What made you come back to the house after you left?"

"I went home and started to do my homework," Kyle explained, "but something kept bugging me, and I just couldn't put my finger on it. And then it hit me. You were entirely too nice to me. Something had to be wrong. You've never been that sweet in your entire life."

Then he kissed me again, and I started to be a little glad that I was still alive.

CHAPTER FOURTEEN

"You're looking mighty fine, girl," Kyle told me, as he walked inside my front door.

"Always have, always will," I quipped, but my knees were shaking so bad I thought I would fall over from the vibrations.

It was a week later, early in the morning, and Kyle had just come by to pick me up for school. For my first day back to school, that is. It was still the very last place on God's green Earth I wanted to go.

I knew I was the talk of the junior class, maybe even the whole school. By this time everyone knew I had tried to kill myself, which was a great topper to all the wild rumors running amok. Donna called me once and was kind enough to inform me that no one believed I actually had some kind of arthritis. The AIDS rumor was so rampant as to seem like fact, with the added twist that I had been pregnant, aborted the baby, and then tried to kill myself because I knew I was going to die, anyway. She also told me that rehearsals for Sizzle were going great, that they had their plane tickets for California and the school was giving them a big send-off party. And oh, yes, Richmond and Cassie were an inseparable couple, and Crater was writing love poetry to Lindsey Van Owen and slipping it into her gym bag.

She told me all of this "as a friend," you understand.

I smashed this ugly ceramic kitten that J.J. won for Momma at the Tennessee State Fair against the wall after that phone call, but then I got to thinking. The truth of the matter was, I hadn't been a real friend to Donna, so why should I expect Donna to be a real friend to me? I never even gave much thought to who she really was or how she really felt. I just used her. Actually, I hadn't ever given very much thought to anyone's feelings but my own. "You reap what you sow," is what Kyle said to me. I just hate it when he gets all biblical.

I suppose I always knew, deep in my heart, that

I had to go back and face all those kids, just like Kyle said. If I didn't, they would win. They would have beaten me down, and I couldn't stand that. If I was going to live, I was going to live proud.

"Maybe you need a little more blush, baby," Momma said nervously, hovering over me. She'd gotten up early to help me get ready for school, and if anything she was even more nervous than I was. She'd also pinched her pennies together and somehow had come up with the money to buy me a new sweater, and for once she didn't buy tacky. It was pink angora with a sweetheart neck and full sleeves tapering down to fitted cuffs of lace. It looked like something Suzanne Lafayette would wear. Tears came to my eyes when she showed me that sweater—it was so obviously something she never would have purchased for herself. She was trying so hard, and she loved me so much.

"I don't need more blush," I told Momma and fluffed my hair up a little in the mirror. My hair looked as wild as ever, which I thought was a nice contrast with the demure-looking sweater. Below that I wore a short pink denim skirt and cowboy boots. There was only so far I was willing to go in the looks-like-something-Suzanne-would-wear category.

I picked up my book bag and slung it over my shoulder. The pain was somewhat better now—I could carry things for short periods of time without being in agony. I still needed the cane, though, so I picked it up and resolutely headed for the door.

"Knock 'em dead, baby," Momma said, and gave me a big kiss.

"Absolutely," I assured her as I limped out.

I was okay for the first half of the trip, but once we got within a few miles of school I started to shake all over. Kyle put his hand over mine and didn't say a word.

When we parked in the parking lot, I saw a few kids I knew standing around talking. As soon as they got a glimpse of me they began whispering furiously. At that moment I wanted to jump right back into Kyle's car, but he took my arm and I knew I wasn't alone.

"It always was you and me against the world," he whispered in my ear. I managed a smile, and we made our way slowly towards the front door of the school.

Kyle opened the front door for me and I walked in. As usual kids were running around, talking, yelling, laughing. And then it seemed as if there was some unspoken cue, and one by one they turned and saw me standing there at the door, leaning on my cane, and just like in a movie the noise became a murmur, and then there was silence. Kyle reached for my arm.

"No," I said, and shook him off. I took a deep breath, tossed my hair back and held my head up high. Then I slowly limped my way down the hall.

Here's where the movie part stops. In a movie, they'd have all the kids respect me right about now, and one kid would applaud, and then a few more would join in, until finally everyone in the hallway would be clapping and cheering for me, and I'd know I was accepted and still loved.

That didn't happen.

People started whispering and talking again, some pointing at me, some being more furtive, but no one made a move to speak to me. I pretended not to care.

Kyle kissed me good-bye on the cheek in front of the biology lab, and I limped in and sat at my desk.

"Hey!" said Donna with a big, fake smile when she saw me.

"Hey," I replied, and opened my biology book.

"I told my mom about your arthritis," Donna said, "and she told me you need to see a psychic herbalist." She took a paper out of her purse and handed it to me. "Here's his name. My mom says he cures arthritis all the time, so you should call him. I mean, he got rid of all her cellulite!"

"Rheumatoid arthritis can't be cured by a psychic herbalist," I explained patiently. Dr. Major's nurse had warned me that people with R.A. often got all kinds of unsolicited advice from people about "cures," usually based on a total lack of knowledge about the disease.

"Oh, I get it," Donna said, nodding her head wisely. "You don't think you'll be able to afford him."

"It doesn't have anything to do with that—" I began.

"Maybe he takes charity cases," she said with a shrug. "Or I could ask my mom if we could help you out!"

It was everything I could do not to slap her. Was she always this callous and crass? "Not interested," I managed, and stared hard at my biology text.

The day went downhill from there. The kids who thought I had AIDS walked as far away from me as possible. No one spoke to me, except to offer suggestions on how I should cure myself. One girl gave me a pamphlet from something called the Christian Mind Society that stated that a man in New York had cured himself of AIDS through positive thinking. I threw it in the trash can.

By lunchtime I was ready to give up. I was exhausted from limping from class to class, and I didn't think I could stare into one more pitying face. Then Kyle came up to me in the lunch room and wrapped his arms around me tenderly, and for a moment I just wanted to fall over, to let him make everything okay for me.

"I can't do this, Kyle!" I whispered into his chest.

"Yes, you can," he told me. "You're the strongest, bravest person I've ever met in my life."

"But they all hate me," I protested.

"Amber-Lynn, they don't even know you," he told me. "You never let them."

"Maybe I'm not worth knowing," I confessed, tears threatening to spill over.

"And maybe you are," he said tenderly. "But sure enough they ain't gonna make the first move. It's gonna have to be you, baby."

I looked into his eyes and all I saw was love. Kyle Gaines knew all my secrets, he knew I couldn't dance anymore, and he loved me still. If someone as wonderful as him could know the real me and still love me, maybe, just maybe, I really was worth knowing.

Kyle went to get us both lunch, and I looked around the lunch room. As usual people were staring at me, gawking and whispering. I saw Richmond with his arms around Cassie, giggling over some private joke. Then over in the corner I saw Bitsy Renfrey sitting by herself, reading a book and eating lunch. At first all I noticed was that she had on a truly terrible outfit that emphasized all the parts she should be trying to hide, but then a funny thing happened.

She looked over at me and she smiled.

Then Bitsy gave the smallest nod, inviting me to come join her. Bitsy Renfrey, the girl I had disdained and made fun of, the girl I would ordinarily never sit with, was inviting *me* to sit with *her*. I gulped hard and slowly limped across the room.

"Hi," I said quietly.

"Have a seat," Bitsy offered.

I sat down across from her.

"So, how are you doing?" she asked me.

"Oh, fine," I began breezily. And then I stopped. Kyle's words replayed themselves in my mind. *You never let them know you.* I took a deep breath. "No, that's not true," I admitted. "I'm not fine. My joints hurt and it's taking all my energy just to drag myself around to my classes."

For a moment Bitsy looked surprised, and then she put her hand on mine and she smiled.

Oh, I was ready for it to be pity, and I was ready to tell her just what she could do with her pity, only it wasn't pity I saw on her face. It was caring. And friendship. Friendship I had never earned from Bitsy Renfrey.

"If you need any help, just let me know," she said sincerely.

"Why are you being nice to me?" I asked her. "I was never very nice to you."

She laughed. "Maybe because I know what it

feels like to be the outsider," she said. "Anyway, I've always really admired you."

"Because of my dancing," I said bitterly.

"No, because of your brain," she replied. "I remember that essay you wrote last year in English that the teacher read out loud, about teens and the politics of class consciousness? And I remember thinking: 'Wow, this girl has a terrific mind.'"

I shrugged. "I just wanted to ace the class, that's all."

"Have you thought about doing any more writing?" she asked me, biting into an apple.

"No," I said bluntly.

"Well, you should," Bitsy said. "You really have talent."

"Are you, like, throwing me a bone because I can't dance anymore?" I asked her sullenly.

"No, I'm just telling you the truth," Bitsy said. "Look, I'm no saint. You're right—you and your friends weren't ever very nice to me. And one part of me wished I could be a part of your group—that's why I tried out for Sizzle," she admitted.

"You were very good," I told her.

"I was?" she asked, her face momentarily lighting up.

I nodded.

"Wow, that's nice," she said with a grin. "But anyway, I used to always think: 'Amber's smarter than they are. I wonder why she hangs out with them?' I figured it had to be because you were so insecure."

As usual a protest came to my lips—I didn't hang out with them, they hung out with me. I wasn't insecure, I was much too cool to be insecure. But that was all lies, and I was trying so hard to tell the truth. On the other hand, you can't get all intimate with someone you don't know very well just because you're trying be honest. So I didn't lie, but I didn't tell her she was dead-on right, either. I just didn't say anything at all. But I knew that she knew.

"Luncheon is served," Kyle said, setting a tray down and slipping in next to me. "How's it goin', Bitsy?"

She blushed and took another bite of her apple. "Oh, you know . . ." she mumbled between chews.

It was then that I remembered they had been a short-lived item earlier in the year, and I had been jealous and hateful about it. Bitsy saw the look on my face, swallowed the apple and smiled at me.

"Don't worry, Amber, I'm not jealous," she said.

"You're very direct, aren't you," I told her.

"Well, sure," she said with a shrug. "Kyle used to talk about you all the time, and I knew he was in love with you. Mostly we were just buddies."

"You're a gracious lady," Kyle told her.

"Oh, well . . ." Bitsy brushed it off. I could see in her face that she was only telling the partial truth—she wished they could have been more than buddies.

"I have to run down to *The Bard* office to do some final edits," Bitsy said, gathering up her stuff. "You ought to think about doing some writing for *The Bard,* Amber," she added. "We could really use your help. See ya."

"Did you really talk about me all the time when you were dating her?" I asked Kyle.

"Yep," he replied, biting into a tuna fish sandwich. "I said you were a snot, a pain in the butt—"

"Gee, thanks!"

"Don't mention it," he replied breezily.

I watched Bitsy walking out of the lunch room. "She's a really nice person, and I never knew it," I said.

"There's a lot of nice kids at this school," Kyle said, "you just weren't hanging out with them."

"You think I can write?" I asked Kyle.

"We used to write songs together all the time," Kyle reminded me. "Besides, I think you can do anything."

"That's not true anymore," I said sadly. "I can't dance. I can't run. I can't even walk without a limp."

"You're right," Kyle amended. "Okay, I think you can do anything that doesn't involve physical fitness."

"That's not how I want it to be," I said in a small voice.

"I know, baby, but that's just the way it is," Kyle said matter-of-factly. "You can't control the cards you're dealt. You can only control the way you play the hand."

"When did you get so smart?" I asked him.

"Just born brilliant, I reckon," he replied airily. "So how about if after school you meet me at *The Bard* office? There's something there I want to show you."

"I don't want to go to *The Bard* office," I groaned. "The dweebs hang out at *The Bard* office."

"Dweebs like me, I guess," Kyle said, finishing his sandwich.

"Well, you're different," I allowed.

"So are you," Kyle stated, "and it's about time you grew up enough to realize it."

"I do not need a lecture from you, Kyle Gaines," I said huffily.

"Just meet me there after school, okay?" he said, and picked up his tray.

"Aren't you going to wait for me?" I asked him, surprised.

"Evidently not," he said, walking away from me.

"I'm not saying I'm meeting you, you know," I called after him.

He just shrugged his shoulders and kept on walking.

All afternoon I told myself that I wasn't going to meet Kyle. I was really ticked that he had just walked away from me like that. On the other hand, he had the car and I didn't have any other way to get home. I told myself that was the only reason I was going to show up.

By the time the school day ended and I dragged myself to *The Bard* office I was feeling like chopped meat gone bad. All I wanted to do was crawl into bed and go to sleep. But I forced myself to stop in the ladies' room and fix my makeup and my hair. Feeling near death is no excuse to let yourself go.

When I got to the office, Bitsy was there. As soon as she saw me, she smiled brightly, like she was happy to see me.

"I'm supposed to meet Kyle here," I told her, not feeling like sharing in her perkiness.

"Oh, sure," she said. "He's in the back room doing a layout. So have you thought about doing some writing?"

"Not really," I said. I sat down in the nearest chair, too tired to stand up any longer.

"Suit yourself," she said with a shrug, then went back to the article she was editing.

I watched her for a while as she crossed out some words and wrote others in the margin. "Look, if I were going to write something, what would I write?" I finally asked her.

She looked up at me. "It's a literary magazine. Why would I tell you what you should write? That has to come from inside *you*."

"I see you decided to show up," Kyle said with a grin, walking over to us.

"I needed a ride home," I mumbled, stiffly getting up from the chair.

"Come on, I want to show you something," he said. I limped beside him into the back office. No one else was back there. He took me in his arms and gave me a soft, melting kiss.

"That's what you wanted to show me?" I asked him.

"Among other things," he nodded. "Look at this." He pointed to a bulletin board on the wall, which was covered with notices, scraps of paper, and various schedules.

"A bulletin board," I said. "Lovely. Can we go home now?"

"No, I mean *this*." He pointed to a blue piece of paper up in the corner. It was a notice from a publishing house in New York City, announcing a contest for high school students.

Puffin Books announces the **It Happened To Me** *Contest for high school students. We are seeking manuscripts from students, ages 15–18, written in first person, which tell the true story of a personally challenging experience that has affected the writer's life. The winning entry will receive $1,000 and have her/his manuscript published by Puffin.*

The notice went on to give more details, such as length of manuscript and deadlines for entry.

"So?" I said.

"So you're in the process of having a challenging experience that is affecting your life," Kyle said.

"Oh, please, Kyle," I snorted. "I am not writing some sob story to send in to some stupid contest."

"What's stupid about it?" he asked mildly.

"Why don't I just go on *Oprah* and let the whole world gawk at me?" I yelled. "I hate this!"

"Fine, then, don't do it," Kyle said, sounding irritated.

"I won't!"

"Good, don't!"

"Can we go home now?"

"Fine!" he bellowed. "You want to remind me again why I love you?"

"Because of my sweet nature!" I snapped, and limped out of the back office as quickly as my pathetic legs could carry me.

CHAPTER FIFTEEN

Kyle and I barely spoke on the way home. I knew I was being hateful, but I couldn't seem to stop myself. I just felt so angry about everything. I didn't want to have this horrid disease! I wanted things to be like they were before.

"Well, baby, how was it?" Momma asked when I limped in the front door. She had taken off work for my first day back to school.

"Grand," I told her sarcastically. "They're nominating me for homecoming queen."

"How about you lay down and I'll fix you a nice cup of cocoa?" Momma asked, an anxious smile on her face.

I was too tired to even answer her. I just limped into the bedroom and fell on the bed. I must have fallen asleep before she could make the cocoa, because when I woke up it was dark out and I was laying there in my rumpled school outfit.

"Momma?" I called to her.

"You fell asleep," she said softly, standing in the doorway. "Feel better?"

"My new sweater is all mussed," I said, looking down at myself.

"Oh, it don't matter, sweet pea," Momma said kindly. "It'll hang out. Here, let me help." She carefully lifted off my sweater and laid it over the edge of the chair. I slipped out of my skirt, and she handed me a big T-shirt that she helped me pull over my head. "Better?"

I nodded. "Thanks, Momma."

She sat on the edge of the bed. "I have a surprise for you, baby," she said. "It's from J.J."

"A black eye?" I asked sardonically.

"Oh, baby, he doesn't do things like that anymore," Momma assured me. "He's a changed human being."

"Look, I'm really not interested in any surprise from J.J., Momma, no offense," I told her.

"You don't even know what it is yet," Momma said in this real pleading kind of voice.

"Go ahead," I said grudgingly.

"Well, Kyle told me maybe you would start doing some writing—" Momma began.

"When did he tell you that?" I demanded.

"A couple of days ago," Momma said. "Something about a contest, he said."

"Why that lowlife scum sucker!" I thundered. "He didn't even tell me about that contest until today! Who the hell does he think he is, planning my life?"

"Well, I'm sure I don't know, Amber-Lynn," Momma said, her hands fluttering around in that nervous way she had.

"Go on," I said grimly.

"Well, I mentioned this to J.J. last night when he stopped in to see me at work," Momma continued anxiously. "And then while you were asleep just now, he brought you by a present. It's used, he says, but it works." Momma disappeared into the living room and came back into the bedroom with an electric typewriter. She set it on the nightstand and looked at me hopefully.

"J.J. got me this?"

Momma nodded. "From a second-hand store." She plugged it in and stuck a piece of paper in it, then poked the keys with one fake nail. "See?"

"But J.J. hates me," I protested.

"Oh, no he doesn't, sugar," Momma said. "He thinks you hate him."

"Well, I do," I told her.

"You should give him a chance," Momma said softly. "He's going to them A.A. meetings now. He's been sober for one month."

"Big deal," I scoffed. Momma's face looked so hurt, though, that I couldn't stand it. "Okay, it's a start," I added. "And I guess I can use the typewriter for homework assignments."

"But Kyle said—"

"I don't care what Kyle said," I interrupted. "Kyle is full of it."

"Hey, ya'll!" a male voice called from the front of the house. "Anyone home?"

"Well, speak of the devil," I said, recognizing Kyle's voice.

"I'll let him in," Momma said eagerly, patting the cotton-candy poof that passed for her hair.

"How you doin', angel face?" Kyle asked, leaning over and giving me a kiss.

"I thought we were fighting," I reminded him.

"Why bother?" he asked, and kissed me again.

"Not so fast, Bubba," I told him. "Why did you tell Momma I was going to start writing and enter some contest before you even mentioned it to me, and before I said I had any interest in it, which I don't?"

"Try to work on those run-on sentences of yours," Kyle said, sitting down next to me on the bed. He looked down at my legs peeking out of the bottom of my long T-shirt. "They might not work so well right now," he said appreciatively, "but dang if they don't look as fine as ever."

"We're not talking about my legs here," I informed him. "I'm not entering that contest."

"Okay," he said, and pushed some hair off my face.

"I mean it, Kyle. I'm not hanging out my dirty laundry for the world to have a good look-see."

"I don't think getting sick and learning to cope with it is exactly dirty laundry, but like I said, okay," Kyle said with a friendly shrug.

"And I'm not learning to cope, either," I said irritably. "I sound like a heroine in some damn soap opera."

"Okay, you're not writing and you're not learning to cope," Kyle said, nodding. "Anything else?"

"Yes. Quit being so nice," I groused. "It makes me very suspicious."

"I can't help it," Kyle said. "I feel great."

"How come?" I asked suspiciously.

"Well, I got home and I was so danged mad at you I wanted to throttle you—"

"Don't give me that sexist swill!" I exploded.

"But at the same time, I got this real happy feeling. And finally I figured it out. You were being your old, impossible self again! Only difference was, now you were mine, and I just got this big ole grin on my face."

"Is that right?" I asked him in a low voice.

"That's right," Kyle answered, and gave me the most impossibly fabulous kiss any girl ever experienced.

"Janet Jackson is going to be at Middle Tennessee Saturday night," he told me. "Want to go?"

"Since when can you afford concert tickets?" I asked him.

"Since Covington got tickets so someone could review the show for the school paper," he said. "I recommended you, and I thought you might could take me."

I laughed. "That's very nice of me."

"Yeah, it's that sweet nature of yours," he said solemnly, and leaned over for another kiss. "Pick you up in the morning," he said, and sauntered out.

I limped out into the kitchen for a glass of juice. Momma was at the stove making dinner.

"He grew up real nice, didn't he," Momma said, as she watched him leave.

"He'll do," I said, opening the refrigerator.

"Oh, you can't fool me about love, sweet pea," Momma said. "You're in love with that boy. And he's in love with you."

"Maybe," I said, sipping the juice.

"Shoot, I've known it for years," Momma said. "Seems like it took the two of you forever to figure it out."

I had to laugh at that. I went over to Momma and I kissed her cheek. "I love you, Momma."

"And I love you, baby. I always will."

"Guess I'll go do my homework," I said, and headed back into the bedroom.

I figured I'd start with geometry, getting the worst out of the way first. I had written the assignment on a piece of paper that I'd stuck in my purse, so I sat on my bed and rummaged through it.

And there was the blue paper announcing the *It Happened To Me* Contest. Kyle must have slipped it into my purse while he was sitting on my bed. He was purely impossible.

I sat on the edge of my bed, reading over that notice. What if Bitsy and Kyle were right, and I really was a good writer? I got A's on all my papers, but it just never mattered to me that much. Still, what if I had it in me to be really good, great even? Great writers had a lot of power, didn't they? And couldn't a great writer maybe win a scholarship to college and after that get rich and famous? Wasn't it just possible that I could express all that was inside of me with words instead of movement?

Of course, I could fail miserably, too.

Well, that was just a chance I would have to take.

And so with Travis Tritt singing "I'm Gonna Be Somebody" on the radio, and the smell of Momma's god-awful hamburgers frying in the kitchen, and the taste of Kyle's kiss still on my lips, I put a piece of paper into the typewriter and turned on the power.

And I began to write.

"On the first day of my junior year of high school, I made Richmond Remington the Third kiss me right in front of Suzanne Lafayette's locker. . . ."

About the Author

Cherie Bennett is one of the best-selling young adult novelists in the country, and is also a screenwriter and award-winning playwright. She lives with her husband, theatrical and film producer Jeff Gottesfeld, in Nashville, Tennessee.

It should be the time of your life, but sometimes it's not easy

F ew authors write so convincingly about real life problems as does Cherie Bennett. Why? Because she's been there. She knows. Each book in her inspiring new series focuses on one girl whose destiny is forever changed by a wrenching life crisis, from a crippling illness to the public indiscretions of a prominent parent to the loss of a sibling. How the *Surviving Sixteen* heroines face and ultimately overcome their challenges is what sets them apart and makes these stories so compellingly readable.

The Fall of the Perfect Girl
(September, 1993)

You can't stay Daddy's little girl forever—as Suzanne Lafayette is about to find out when a scandal involving her father explodes her safe little world.

A beautiful young girl, a full moon, and a mysterious stranger waiting in the woods . . .

Ann Hodgman's stunning new **CHILDREN OF THE NIGHT** series debuts in October with . . .

DARK DREAMS

Something Lila no longer even remembers, something that happened when she was only a child, is about to shatter her world and direct her destiny. A childhood attack by a wolf has returned to haunt her, and now, in her sixteenth year, an incredible transformation is taking place: Lila's discovered she's a werewolf. Desperately hiding her secret, Lila has never felt so alone. But there is someone out there who longs to help her—if only she'll trust him.

THE DARK CARD

Laura thinks she's playing to win
. . . but at what cost?

Laura loves the flashiness and glamour of the casinos. When she sits at the blackjack table, dressed in silken clothes and beautiful jewelry, she feels like a sophisticated woman of the world. But Laura is living a double life, and it's about to catch up with her.